# Courting the Consequences

## Ravager Knights MC Book 1

M. E. Thornwood

Midnight Dreaming Publishing

Midnight Dreaming Publishing
P.O. Box 312
Elburn, IL 60119



Interior design by Atticus

Book Cover by Covers by Jules

Edited by Maine Woods Editing

ISBN 978-1-962688-01-7

ISBN 978-1-962688-00-0 (ebook)

*Courting the Consequences is book one of the Ravager Knights MC series. It will end in a cliff hanger with the HEA at the end of book three.*

*This is a Why Choose novel, meaning the main character will not choose between her love interests. This novel has BDSM themes and on page negotiations.*

*If rough sex, degradation, and angry alpha males that fly off the handle is not your cup of tea, please don't read.*

*This is a work of fiction intended for an 18+ audience.*

To Me.

For following your dreams and making them come true.

# Contents

# Chapter One

"YOU CAN'T FUCKING FIRE me! I made this firm! I started it with your father!" Ken Laraway screamed as he stormed into her office.

"Sure, Ken, come on in, 'cause I'm not busy," Kara Carmichael drawled as he stomped toward her desk.

His red face contrasted with his white hair. His gut hung over his ill-fitting suit pants, and the buttons on his shirt strained. He looked like an overgrown gorilla... And he thought he was God's gift to women?

Kara narrowed her eyes at the man ranting and raving in front of her. She leaned back in her plush desk chair and crossed her right leg over her left. She smoothed the hemline of her pencil skirt and took her time looking back up at the man who was spitting with rage across the wooden desk from her.

Men like Ken Laraway really didn't like a woman in charge and often overcompensated by trying to demean and belittle them.

Years of courtroom etiquette had Kara schooling her features when she really wanted to snap at the senior partner.

Instead, she slowly got to her feet. She buttoned up her own suit jacket and glanced behind Ken to the open door. Her eleven o'clock was right on time. A tall blond man stood out in the waiting area near her secretary. Dressed in dark blue jeans and a suit coat, he gave off a professional yet casual air. The scowl on his handsome face as he blatantly stared into her office suggested he would intervene should she need it.

"Mr. Laraway," Kara started as she rounded her desk, "I think you'll find that I absolutely can and will fire you for just cause."

"Just cause?" Ken spat. "That little slut is lying. I never came on to her. I don't even know her name. Why would I want some twenty-something bimbo? I'm a married man."

Kara groaned internally. There were so many things she wanted to say to that. But she couldn't. Not if she wanted this firing to stick legally; and she needed it to stick legally. Ken Laraway was just another one of her father's old-time crew that were all the same. Backward thinking, misogynistic, and *loyal to her father*.

"Mr. Laraway, we have video footage of you entering the women's bathroom and cornering her against the wall. This is not a case of her word against yours; we have just cause. You'll find in the bylaws—that you and my father wrote together back in

1986—that sexual harassment is a fire-able offense." Kara stood in front of her desk and rested her ass on the edge, leaning back and crossing her arms over her chest.

"Your father bringing you into this firm was the biggest mistake he ever made. You think that all this new age mumbo jumbo will last? This is still a man's world, whether you like it or not." Ken slowly stalked toward her. "Your father should have left you in the ghetto he found you in," he growled harshly.

Kara chuckled softly, half in disbelief, half in irony. She pushed away from the desk, needing to be on her feet for this argument. "Maybe so, Mr. Laraway. But that is none of your business. You have been fired for sexual harassment. Section 8 of the bylaws states that no employee will retain employment after evidence has been presented in the case of sexual harassment. All judgments will be made by the human resource—"

"I know what the damn bylaws say! I fucking wrote them!" he screamed in her face.

Movement behind Laraway caught her eye. Her eleven o'clock had moved into her office, slowly and quietly. Her distraction was the opening Ken Laraway needed. He reached out, wrapped his hand around her throat, and squeezed.

"Hey!" the man shouted from near the door. He moved forward quickly to grab Laraway.

Kara didn't hesitate. She slammed her knee into Laraway's balls, and he fell back gasping.

She took a deep breath and shook her head, regaining her composure. "You'll find that HR has already cleared your desk of your personal belongings. Security will escort you out." She motioned to two very large and intimidating security guards that had just stepped into the waiting area outside her office.

Security made quick work of picking up Ken Laraway from the floor and escorting him out. The silence left behind was deafening. Kara sighed and leaned back against her desk, resting her ass on the edge.

"Are you OK?" her would-be rescuer asked, his voice deep.

Kara looked over at him. He had short blond hair, longer on top and styled into the spiky bedhead look. Piercing baby-blue eyes above high chiseled cheekbones. His strong jaw was covered in a trimmed blond beard. He was tall and broad. The black blazer he wore over a navy button-up barely contained the muscles he was clearly rocking. Clean, dark wash jeans and a pair of brown cowboy boots completed the look. He was smoking hot.

"Yes," Kara answered after her quick perusal. "Sorry about the drama. It's not usually so exciting around here." She stepped forward and offered her hand. "Kara Carmichael."

"Johnathan Taylor. Taylor Construction and Mechanical." His deep voice was a rumble in her soul. His hand was callused and warm, his grip firm but gentle. "Are you sure you're OK, ma'am?"

His concern was heartwarming. She nodded, "Yes, I'm fine." She squeezed his fingers before quickly dropping his hand and turning away. "And thank you for not stepping in. It would have gotten messy if you had."

"I was about to when he put his hands on you, but you handled it just fine." He gave her a proud smile that had a shiver running down her spine.

"Well thank you, Mr. Taylor. I appreciate that," she said as she rounded her desk.

"Johnny, please," he said as he walked toward the chairs set in front of her desk.

Kara sighed and took a seat. She reached down into a lower desk drawer and pulled out a bottle of Macallan and two glasses. She didn't even ask him before she poured him two fingers alongside hers. She put the cap back on the bottle and slid the other glass to Johnny as she took a sip.

He frowned as he reached for his glass. "You accustomed to drinking before noon at the office?"

She looked up into his intense baby-blue eyes and raised her glass. "I'm not accustomed to being choked by douchebags unless I've given consent."

"Fair enough," he smirked and took a sip of the whisky. "That's smooth," he commented, licking his lips.

"Macallan," she answered with a shrug. "Alright, Johnny." She smiled and leaned back in her chair. "I'll be honest. I was expecting Scott Wallen and your design team today. I'm a little surprised to see the boss himself."

Johnny shrugged. "I figured the designs were drawn up, all that was left was to present them to you and sign paperwork."

"So you thought you'd come reel in the big fish yourself?" she smirked, raising an eyebrow.

"Something like that," he grinned.

"Alright, let's see these designs."

He took another sip of his whisky before he reached down beside his chair. "Ah, I left my laptop out there. I'll be back."

She nodded and stood up. She watched him go and admired the way his ass filled out his jeans before she grabbed both of their glasses and headed to the conference table in the corner of her office. She set down both glasses as Johnny walked back in with a laptop bag slung over his shoulder. He set up quickly and started showing her his company's designs for the remodeling of the Carmichael building.

Two hours later the two finished the Italian they had ordered in for lunch. As Johnny reached across the table to help Kara clean up their food, there was a loud ripping sound.

"Fuck," Johnny swore, looking annoyed.

Kara looked up from her food in alarm. "Are you OK? What happened?"

Johnny nodded, looking slightly sheepish as he glanced over his shoulder. "Sorry ma'am. I think my jacket just ripped."

Kara tried not to smile as she looked over his shoulder and saw the rip down the middle of the jacket. "Oh yeah," she chuckled lightly, "that's what you get for trying to contain those muscles."

Johnny smiled and shrugged.

"Take it off," she ordered as she got up and walked toward her desk. "I'll get you the number of my tailor. Do yourself a favor and get at least one tailor-made jacket for clients."

"Yeah, not really my style," Johnny rebuffed.

She rolled her eyes but grabbed a business card out of her desk drawer. She turned back around to see him folding the coat over the back of one of the conference table chairs. His navy button-up shirt was straining against his biceps. "Let me guess, you're more a T-shirt and jeans man," Kara cocked a brow.

He grinned and nodded, eyes on her as she walked toward him.

"Well, get at least *one* suit tailor-made for client meetings. You'll realize quickly how stuff off the rack just doesn't fit the same. Trust me, all of *this* does *not* fit into off-the-rack clothing," she drawled, motioning to the very ample chest that God and her momma had given her.

For the first time since meeting the man, Kara noticed him glance down at her chest. Her blouse was red silk and buttoned high enough to be considered professional but still show a hint of cleavage. It fit well, and the black jacket she had on accented her body and slimmed down some of her curves.

Johnny smirked and his baby blues darkened with desire as his gaze returned to hers. "No, I imagine it doesn't." His voice was husky and deep.

Kara smiled coyly, licking her lips subconsciously as she got lost in his eyes. Even in her six-inch heels, he towered over her, easily a foot taller. She held out the card, and he reached for it, fingers brushing hers.

*Goddamn this man is sex on wheels.*

"Listen—," Johnny started.

"I'm sorry to interrupt, Miss Carmichael, but your father is on line one," Stacy, her secretary, said over the intercom.

Kara schooled her features and composed herself. "Of course," she muttered. "Thank you, Stacy." She turned to Johnny, "I'm sorry to cut this short, but I need to take this."

He nodded, his stare penetrating her soul. "Of course."

She grabbed her cell phone off the conference table and rushed out of her office. "Stacy, put him through to my cell," she told her secretary and headed down the hall.

"This is Kara," she answered as she hit the stairwell, already knowing damn well who was on the phone.

"What the fuck is this I hear about you firing Ken Laraway?" Vince Carmichael screeched in her ear.

Kara rolled her eyes. Her father did like dramatics, especially when he didn't get his way. "Afternoon, Dad, how's your day going?" Kara greeted as she started heading down the stairs from the thirtieth floor.

"Don't bullshit me right now. This isn't a game. This is a man's livelihood we're talking about," her father ranted.

"He should have fucking thought about that before he sexually harassed one of my employees, *before* he wrapped his hand around my goddamn throat," she shouted back as she reached the landing. She turned and headed down the next set of stairs.

She found Kevin Adams—a contract employee and electrician for Taylor Construction and Mechanical—on a ladder fixing a lighting fixture on the landing below. He looked up at her with rage immediately simmering in his dark eyes.

She paused, realizing she wasn't alone in the stairwell.

Of all the people to run into, though, she was glad it was Kevin. They had developed an easy friendship over his three-year tenure with her company. The Carmichael building was on his regular rotation, and he stopped in anywhere from once a week to everyday depending on what the facilities department needed.

It had been because of his great work that she had considered hiring the company he worked for to do the remodeling project. It only made sense to keep things in house, so to speak.

Her father was silent for a moment. "He did WHAT?" he screamed.

Kara sighed and continued down the stairs. Kevin climbed down his ladder. His dark spiky hair glistened in the florescent lighting. He was tall and broad-shouldered, well built, with dark brown eyes that were gentle and kind. He wore a black T-shirt and a pair of blue jeans with his work boots. He was easy on the eyes and very sweet.

Kara enjoyed running into him on the days he was in the building.

"Look Dad, I can't really talk right now. I'll call you later tonight, alright?" Kara tried to get her father off the phone quickly.

"Make sure that you do," he snapped before ending the call.

*Thanks for asking if I'm alright, Dad.*

Kara locked her screen as she came to a stop before Kevin. "Are you alright?" he asked immediately. His hand came up to her jaw, cupping it gently as he lifted her face up and tilted it out of the way so the light would shine on her neck.

"I'm fine," she murmured softly, eyes on his. His chocolate orbs were so dark they were almost black with his rage.

When he didn't look convinced, she set her hand on his wrist. "I'm OK," she said again, slightly squeezing.

His eyes finally met hers, and she could see the torment raging behind his gaze, feel the tension between them. There was always tension between them.

This was one of those defining moments; one little kiss could change it all. One little kiss that she couldn't afford to give him. At least not in the office. There were cameras everywhere. He was a contract employee. There were no rules stating they couldn't date, but she didn't need it getting out that she was making out with someone in the stairwell. She was the boss, a title most had felt was handed to her because her father owned the business.

She didn't like giving the firing squad any more ammunition.

She was still rattled, though, from her encounter with Laraway, not to mention the sexual tension between her and Johnny that had been palpable. Now, with Kevin, she was feeling vulnerable. She moved before he could and pressed herself against him. She wrapped her arms around his waist, burying her face in his chest.

His arms came around her instantly. He smelled heavenly, of mint and leather. There was a hint of something metallic to his scent, probably from whatever electrical work he had been doing. She inhaled deeply and felt one of his hands rest on her lower back, while the other slid to the nape of her neck. He held her tightly as he rested his chin on the top of her head.

Kara had never felt so safe.

Kevin Adams couldn't believe he actually had her in his arms. He had been dying for this moment since the first time he saw her three years ago when he was first hired on as a contract employee to keep up with all their electrical needs. He'd watched from afar until one day they had started their playful banter. Now he could almost admit she was a friend or acquaintance in the office. She was genuine and down to earth and seemed to actually care about the people that worked for her.

She trembled slightly against him and he had to fight back a groan. Her body was soft and luscious against his. Her blond hair smelled of vanilla and cinnamon.

He heard a light scuffing on the steps above them. He looked up to see his boss and best friend, Johnny Taylor, watching the two of them with an unreadable look on his face.

Kevin was surprised to see him. He knew he'd had a meeting with Kara to finalize the plans for her upcoming remodel. Johnny had made it seem like they would just be signing papers and then starting next week. Today was supposed to have been a formality, but something was clearly up.

"What happened?" Kevin asked Kara, his eyes on his boss and best friend.

Kara shook her head against his chest. "Just a disgruntled employee I had to let go today."

"It wasn't nothing. He choked her," Johnny growled as he came down the steps, always the hothead.

Kara froze in Kevin's arms; obviously she'd been unaware he was behind her. She jumped back from Kevin like she'd been burned and shot her gaze to Johnny's.

Johnny's hands came up in surrender and he slowed his approach.

Kevin groaned internally. He already missed the heat of her soft body pressed against his.

"Didn't mean to startle you," Johnny said slowly. "I thought you might be upset after the call from your father."

Kara looked slightly unnerved. "I'm fine," she muttered. "I'll meet you back in my office in ten minutes," she said with a more authoritative air.

Johnny nodded and slowly lowered his arms.

Kara nodded, then stepped past Kevin without looking at him and exited the stairwell using the door to the twenty-seventh floor.

Once the door was closed, Kevin turned back to his best friend. "What the fuck happened?"

"Fucking bullshit. Some old fucker cornered a woman in the bathroom. She went to HR, he was canned, but he came storming into Kara's office bitching a fit," Johnny shook his head in disbelief. "She's tough as shit, though. I'll give her that. She never backed down when he came in screaming, and she stood up to him for being a sleaze. Started spouting back at him about bylaws and shit. Dude, it was fucking hot."

Kevin rolled his eyes. "And the choking?"

"I was in the hallway, so I couldn't hear all of it, but he said something that made her laugh, and she said something back that pissed him off. I was trying to get closer when she saw me. She looked away from the guy and he wrapped his hand around her neck. She kneed him in the balls before I could even get across the room."

"Jesus Christ," Kevin swore and ran a hand through his dark hair.

"She's a feisty thing," Johnny smirked. "You hittin' that?"

Kevin narrowed his gaze on his friend. "No, and neither are you if you know what's good for you."

Johnny's shoulders squared and he took a moment to assess Kevin. "I'm just admiring from afar," he drawled.

Kevin rolled his eyes. He knew his buddy all too well. Riling Kevin up was what Johnny lived for. "Don't you have a meeting to get to? Papers to sign?" he prompted.

Johnny grinned. "Sure do, bro. I should go make sure the little spitfire isn't all hot and bothered. That hug looked tempting." Johnny patted him on the shoulder as he walked by. He exited the stairwell through the same door Kara had, a slight pep in his step.

Once the door was closed, Kevin sighed. It would be just his luck if Johnny took interest in Kara too. After all these years Kevin had never made a move, and now he might not get a chance.

Johnny found Kara back in her office ten minutes later. She was sitting at her desk, the contract between their companies on the desk before her. He waited until she finished signing the papers before he made his presence known.

He could see from the doorway that her cool composure was back, the mask of indifference firmly in place. He decided right then and there that he didn't like it. The mask. He'd seen her fiery and passionate. He'd seen her drop her walls and seek comfort.

This *indifference* was not what he wanted to see. At least not while he was around.

"That happen often around here? You and Kevin?" He went straight for the jugular. He was a grab-life-by-the-balls kind of man. There was no sugarcoating with him.

Her eyes snapped to his, and that passionate anger flared to life behind those sky blues. "Excuse me?" she shot out. Her eyes narrowed. Her pouty pink lips pursed.

"You looked awfully cozy down in that stairwell. How do I know you're not taking advantage of my employee?" Johnny goaded, knowing damn well it wasn't like that.

Kara composed herself. That fiery bit of anger he had witnessed was pulled back behind the curtain of indifference. "Kevin is free to go whenever he'd like," Kara stated.

"Not if he's worried that he'd cost his company a big client," Johnny tossed back.

Kara stood from her desk and rounded on him, that mask of indifference slipping. Johnny smirked. *Goddamn, she is hot.* "I know you aren't actually insinuating I would have forced your employee into anything against his will just moments after firing a man for doing the very same thing to one of my employees."

Johnny grinned wickedly, loving how riled up she got. A flush rose over her chest and neck, and her breasts heaved. His cock stirred in his jeans. She had no idea how hot she was all pissed off. "Insinuate? Sure. Believe it? Not a chance. But it was worth it to see that mask you've got in place fall. The ice-queen bit is overplayed," Johnny goaded.

His head snapped to the side from the force of her slap before he even registered that she had moved. A growl ripped out of his chest, and he stepped toward her. Her eyes widened in shock a moment before he grabbed the side of her face and pulled her into a claiming kiss.

She resisted for half a second before she opened those pouty lips and slid her tongue against his. Her hands slid up his chest and neck before they slid through the short hair at his nape. He groaned when she nibbled on his lower lip. His hands wrapped around her trim waist and he lifted her.

She tried to wrap her legs around him, but the damned knee-length pencil skirt she was wearing hindered her.

She cursed and broke away from the kiss, panting.

Johnny set her back down on her desk and leaned his forehead against hers, trying to cool down.

"Why would you say that?" she asked, her sky-blue eyes clouded with worry.

Johnny's eyebrows pulled together, forehead wrinkling against hers.

"About forcing Kevin?" she elaborated.

Johnny smirked against her lips. "Just seeing where you stood with the guy. He's been my best friend since we were kids."

She frowned and pulled away from him. "So you kiss me after seeing me in his arms?"

Johnny moved toward her again. "Like I said, he's been my best friend since we were kids. We're practically brothers. We *share* everything."

He watched her frown. He could see her mind turning over his words, trying to work out what he meant. He kissed her again before she could open her mouth to ask him to clarify.

She gave as good as he took, and he took a lot. Passion and desire flowed between them, a lot of biting and sucking. She was unleashed and it was breathtaking. Johnny couldn't get enough. She tasted like honey, sweet and tangy on his tongue. He bet she tasted even sweeter beneath that skirt.

She broke the kiss, panting. Her chest heaved against his. "I can't," she gasped.

"Why not?" he asked, feeling just a bit rejected.

"For the same reason I never touched Kevin before today. It wouldn't be right."

"Did you sign the contract?" he asked, raising an eyebrow.

"Yes," she murmured.

"Then let me go get Kevin and ask him to join us," Johnny smirked and kissed her again.

She laughed lightly into the kiss before she pushed him away again. "I can't. I'm sorry."

"Alright, Princess," he conceded and pulled back to give her space. "Just lose the ice-queen facade, OK?"

She laughed again. "Don't piss me off again," she shot back.

"Baby, if this is what happens every time I piss you off, you better believe I'll be a thorn in your side from now on," Johnny grinned and adjusted his cock in his jeans.

"So much for the nice guy act," she shot at him.

"Baby, I might be a professional, but I've never been a nice guy," he winked at her.

Kara eyed him and shook her head like she was trying to clear her thoughts. "I can't." She shook her head again. "I can't," she repeated.

"Alright," Johnny shrugged like it was no skin off his back. "If the contract's signed, I'll be out of your hair." He leaned in and pressed an open-mouthed kiss to her neck, sucking deeply.

She let out a low moan.

"You ever change your mind, you know where to find me." Johnny grabbed the signed contract off her desk and turned away. He walked out without glancing back. If he had, if he'd seen how unraveled he'd made her, he might've never left.

# Chapter Two

KEVIN WATCHED HER WALK by without noticing him standing outside a lower-level conference room in the lower atrium. It was a high traffic area as the main thoroughfare to the cafeteria. The sway of her hips had him stirring in his jeans. The black slacks she wore hugged the curve of her ass, accentuated by the six-inch heels she rocked on the daily.

Kevin would know; he watched her enough. *Too much*, his brain supplied.

Today she had on a navy blouse that emphasized her blessed curves. As always, a suit coat completed her look, toning down her tits to a more professional level. Kevin didn't know how she walked around in that getup every day, but he wasn't complaining...her tits were fucking fantastic.

Her blond hair was always coiled in an elegant updo, without a hair out of place. He had never seen it down in the three years he'd been there.

She looked fucking beautiful.

Kevin watched as she walked by while looking down at her phone, lost in thought. "Morning Boss Lady," Kevin greeted.

"Oh," she breathed, hand flying to her heart.

"Sorry, I didn't mean to startle you." He frowned slightly. She wasn't usually so lost in thought. She typically kept her head up and greeted everyone by name as she passed them.

She turned to face him, and a bright smile lit up her face when she saw who it was. "Morning, Kevin. No, it's my fault. I should watch where I'm going. HR has enough safety meetings about this very topic," she laughed lightly, shaking her head.

He smiled and fell into step beside her. "Work just extra busy, or something else got you distracted?" He phished for info. It had been almost three weeks since she hugged him in the stairwell, and in that time, he had barely seen her. He almost thought she was avoiding him.

"No," she shook her head, "I was texting my brother. We're planning a weekend away just the two of us this winter."

"And what does a weekend away look like for a CEO?" Kevin smirked.

She rolled her eyes at him and smiled. "It looks like snowboarding in Pineridge," she answered easily.

Kevin's eyebrows rose in shock. "Well color me surprised," he chuckled. "I'd expect a girl like you to be more into skiing."

"Nah," Kara smirked, "too boring."

Kevin laughed and nodded, "Touché."

"How's your morning going?" she asked, looking up at him. He was almost a foot taller than her. They headed into the cafeteria, her heels clicking with every step.

"Can't complain now that I've gotten to see your beautiful face," Kevin replied, watching her carefully. He had kept his voice low so others around them wouldn't hear.

Her cheeks turned slightly pink as a smile graced her lips. She glanced up at him before looking around. There was no one near them, though they were standing in the middle of the cafeteria. Everyone was minding their own business.

"Could have sworn you might have been avoiding me," Kevin added now that he had her buttered up.

Her smile fell slightly. He could see the emotions warring on her face before she locked them down again and the cool and collected mask slipped into place. She nodded vaguely though, glancing down almost sheepishly. "I might have been," she admitted. Her hands came up to smooth out her suit coat. "I'm sorry," she glanced back up at him.

He furrowed his brow in confusion as he stared down at her. "Why are you apologizing?"

"For avoiding you? I wanted to thank you for being there for me when I was having a moment that day. You were there for me and I appreciated that," she said softly.

Kevin frowned. She sounded like she was talking about a design choice or a meeting agenda, not something as disturbing as being *choked* by an ex-employee and needing to be comforted. "Are you sure you're OK after everything that happened? It's alright to not be OK, you know."

She sighed and glanced around. This really wasn't the fucking place for this conversation. He wanted to take her into his arms and hold her close, tell her he'd take care of her and never let anything bad happen to her again. He couldn't, though.

"I'm honestly OK," she forced a smile on her face and glanced behind him.

"Morning, Miss Carmichael," Kevin heard a woman say from behind him.

"Good morning, Jen," she greeted before turning back to Kevin. "I have to go. It was good to see you again. I'll check in later on the remodel," she gave him a tight smile.

Kevin sighed and nodded, putting on his show. "Have a good day, Miss Carmichael."

# Chapter Three

"Bro, you can't do that here." Derrick "Devil" Halson heard Kevin groan from behind him as he pulled out a cigarette while on the loading dock of the electrical building of Carmichael and Associates. It was his second week on the new job site, and Rockstar had been on his ass all day.

"Chill, I'm heading outside," Derrick replied, tucking the cig behind his ear. He may be new to the job site, but he'd been with Taylor Construction and Mechanical for years. He knew each site had regulations on where employees could smoke, and within those regulations, their own crew generally found places that were acceptable because of who they were. Like when they were on the roof, as long as they didn't leave a mess and had proper ashtrays, no one cared.

For whatever reason, his buddy was extra uptight today. Bro needed to get laid. More and more of their crew had started rolling in over the last several days, and with them, Kevin grew increasingly on edge. He had a good gig going here. Derrick could see why Kevin didn't want their crew screwing up. But they all knew better. Johnny was a hothead on a good day and a bear on a bad day. He drilled jobsite etiquette into all of them.

Derrick led the way out the loading bay door. Just as they stepped out into the blazing May heat, Kara Carmichael herself walked up, looking pinned to perfection. Her perky tits were confined behind a painfully conservative green dress. Conservative to Derrick at least. There was no cleavage shown. And as always, a suit coat covered her arms. Derrick wondered if that was part of the company's dress code, the women having to stay covered like some Stepford wife. God forbid a man see a bit of skin.

"Hey Boss Lady, you're awfully far from your ivory tower. Coming down to mingle with us lowly peasants?" Kevin shot at her. Derrick glanced back at his buddy to see him smiling at Kara.

"Kevin, you know a queen has to be seen mingling with the commoners from time to time," she sneered haughtily, resting her hands on her hips.

Kevin and Derrick laughed easily, but Derrick glanced between the two of them. There was chemistry there for sure, but something else was there too.

She shrugged and smiled sheepishly. "Actually, I was hoping to find you," she hedged. "I might have blown every circuit in my office," she admitted with a wince.

"Oh nooo," Kevin groaned, a smile on his face.

"Nah uh," Derrick chimed in, smile plastered on his face. It was weird watching his bro turn all googly-eyed when this chick was around. "See, this here is a smoke break. You're interrupting a smoke break," he messed with her. He had discovered soon after his arrival at Carmichael and Associates that Miss Carmichael gave as good as she got and liked to have a good time.

She raised an eyebrow at Derrick, not at all impressed. "Well, if you wanna put a nail in your coffin, you go right ahead," she nodded. "But seeing as neither Kevin nor I smoke, we'll just let you do that on your own," she answered.

Derrick opened his mouth to reply, but he had nothing.

A wide grin broke across her face at his loss for words, and Kevin laughed. So, Derrick did what he always did to smart-asses: he flicked her the finger.

"Dude," Kevin immediately hit him in the arm, but Kara laughed deeply, a rich and melodic sound. Derrick decided right then and there he needed to hear it again.

"Forgive me, ma'am," Derrick smiled easily. "I didn't mean to upset your delicate sensibilities," he drawled, knowing damn well she was tougher than that.

Kara laughed and shook her head. "Please, I have none. Not anymore," she shook her head again. "Not in this line of work."

Kevin still shot Derrick a look as Kara turned back toward the main office building. "So, what did you plug in that overloaded the circuit?" Kevin asked as they walked across the parking lot from the electrical building to the main building.

Derrick followed behind them a couple paces so he could stare at her plump ass, juicy round globes that he just wanted to sink his teeth into. It swayed like a dangling fruit before him. He had to stifle a groan. The dress might have had too modest of a neckline for Derrick's liking, but it hugged her body like a glove.

She was fucking beautiful, and Kevin clearly had something going with her, if the flirting was anything to go by.

"A pencil sharpener," she sighed with an embarrassed smile. "I don't even know why I was worried about it. It's not like I use pencils that often."

Kevin smiled, the conversation turned to something else, and Derrick tuned out. He was too busy checking out her ass, the way her hips swung, the flare as they widened before narrowing again at her trim waist. He couldn't see her fucking tits from the back, but he'd love to see them without the fucking suit jackets she always wore.

Before long, they made it to the top floor of the mostly glass Carmichael building. They walked into Kara's office, and Derrick saw the pencil sharpener in question, plugged into a lonely outlet on the wall opposite her desk.

It amazed Derrick how much fucking glass was in the building. The outer walls were mostly all glass, and all the inner hallways on the executive level were glass as well. Kara's desk was on the left side of the room and faced out toward the glass of the hallway. To the right were couches and a couple chairs, a coffee table, end tables, and a rug. There were even lamps on the end tables to make the whole space look warm and inviting. Cozy.

Derrick eyed the office with curiosity while Kevin inspected the outlet and pulled a circuit tester from the pocket of his jeans. He unplugged the pencil sharpener and plugged in the circuit tool. "Alright. I gotta head to the breaker down the hall."

"Thank you, Kevin. I really appreciate it. I'd have called Jamie first, but he left for the day," Kara said.

"No worries. Jamie probably would have called me on this one anyway. The old wiring in this building is still in shambles," Kevin answered with a smile.

"I have a meeting down on six, do you need me, or do you boys got this?" Kara asked with a smile, though Derrick could have sworn there was a mischievous spark in her eye as she looked at the two of them.

Derrick laughed softly and watched as his buddy seemed to stutter over his words, "Uh, yeah, we got this."

He watched her walk away, laptop tucked under her arm, before he turned to his buddy. "Duuuuuude," he groaned.

Kevin shook his head and rolled his eyes. "Don't."

"Bro," Derrick shook his head. "She set that one on a silver platter for you."

Kevin shook his head and walked out of Kara's office.

"How long has it been like that between you two?" Derrick asked as he followed his buddy down the opulent hallway.

"I don't know man, a while. I've been here for years now. We run into each other a lot. She's... *fuck*," he swore, losing his cool. He ran a hand through his hair. "She's outta my league man, but she's fucking amazing."

"She wants to ride that *Rockstar* cock all night," Derrick murmured, well aware it was not the time or place for his bullshit, but he couldn't let his buddy get away unscathed.

Kevin groaned and dropped his head back, looking at the ceiling in disbelief.

Derrick laughed under his breath; his buddy made it too easy to fuck with him sometimes. "You need to get laid, bro."

Kevin just shook his head and pulled open what appeared to be a random door in the hallway that just happened to be a closet with an electrical panel on one wall. *Time to get back to work.*

"Bro, have you seen Rockstar with Carmichael yet?" Derrick asked Johnny one day when he was on-site checking over progress. He'd been away dealing with a mix-up on another job, but he was finally back to help out.

Johnny ran his knuckles over his jaw. "Like today? Or in general?" he asked, blue eyes stony.

"In general, bro," Derrick shook his head, a shit-eating grin on his face. "Dude's in love. I'm calling it now."

Johnny's eyes narrowed quickly. He was a hothead on a good day, and Derrick knew that look. "What do you mean? Have you walked in on them?" he pressed.

Derrick held up his hands in surrender. He'd clearly opened a can of worms he hadn't known about. "Nah man, nothing like that. Just Rockstar's googly-eyed fascination with the chick, their flirty conversations when she's around," Derrick hedged, trying to brush it off.

Johnny smirked and shrugged. "Nah, I haven't. But that sounds like a good show. Rockstar all *googly-eyed*?" he laughed. "That I gotta see."

Derrick laughed and nodded. "For real."

Derrick rounded the corner of the basement storage area that was tucked back behind the loading dock and mail room of the main Carmichael building. They had set up storage in one half of the large room. The other half of the room was being used by the building's facilities department. He wasn't really sure what was on all those pallets, but it wasn't his job to know.

He had come down here looking for a box of nails but heard sniffling from the far end. Clearly someone else was down here. Derrick debated leaving whomever it was alone. But when it turned out that finding that box of nails was harder than finding a damned needle in a haystack, he grew more concerned by the soft female sobbing. He grabbed a roll of paper towels as he passed them and ripped off a bunch.

Derrick considered himself more a love-'em-and-leave-'em type, but he would never intentionally leave a woman in distress. His momma raised him better than that, God rest her soul. So, he headed in search of the crying damsel and was damn glad he had.

Kara Carmichael was sitting on a pile of boxes stacked on a pallet. Her head was in her hands and she was sobbing quietly. *Ah, fuck*, he groaned internally. There was no good way to go about this without startling her. And from what he'd already gathered about her, she was the proud sort and wouldn't accept any assistance he might offer.

It would be better if he turned around and left her alone. Her secrets safe. But he couldn't do that now. His momma raised him right, after all. "Hey there, pretty lady," Derrick murmured softly, not wanting to startle her.

It didn't matter, Kara's head whipped up, and she quickly wiped her eyes.

Derrick held up his hands in surrender. "Hey now, it's alright, I come in peace," he continued. He held out several of the paper towels as an offering of good faith.

Another sob tore out of her as she reached for the paper towels he offered. He moved closer and took a seat beside her. "Bad day?" he asked.

She nodded and wiped her eyes. She took a deep breath in through her nose and held it. When she slowly released it through her mouth, Derrick counted the seconds. Soon he was matching her breathing and counting the seconds, easily recognizing the 4-7-8 breathing technique to ease a panic attack.

When her breathing had calmed, Derrick reached down for the stainless-steel water bottle she carried everywhere with her, one of those insulated ones with a straw. He handed it to her, and she took the heavy bottle with two hands that were slightly shaking.

"Thank you," she murmured softly after she took several sips. She moved to set the bottle back on the ground, but Derrick grabbed it from her and set it down himself.

"Better?" he asked softly.

"A little, thank you," she glanced at him with a watery smile.

He grinned back. She looked fucking beautiful regardless of the tears in her eyes. "Want to talk about it?" he asked.

She smiled wryly and shook her head. "Not really. My father is an asshole, though," she shrugged.

Derrick grinned broadly at her cussing. "Ahh, gotta love the old daddy-problems cliché," Derrick drawled.

Kara shrugged and gently wiped her face. Overall, for just having sobbed her eyes out, she looked mostly put together, minus the watery gaze. Give her another minute, and Derrick was sure she would be as composed and collected as she usually was, put together and with her ice-queen facade, as Johnny called it, firmly in place.

"I'm sorry," he said, realizing how he'd just brushed off her feelings. "I didn't mean to be a dick."

"But you don't know any other setting?" she offered, a small smile on her lips.

He barked a laugh and nodded. "Basically."

She laughed lightly and shrugged. "Every girl has daddy issues if you look hard enough. Some are just bigger than others."

Derrick nodded. "So dear ole dad is a dick?"

Kara laughed and wiped her eyes again. "Not always," she shrugged. She didn't seem to want to get into it, and Derrick respected that.

"Were you close growing up?" he asked, phishing for a way in.

Kara shook her head. "I didn't know him then. I was raised by my mom. Single mother. I didn't meet my dad until I was in college," Kara admitted.

Derrick hung his head, knowing the story all too well. "My mom was alone too. Raised me herself." He sighed and nudged her shoulder with his. "She was amazing."

She leaned into him slightly, pressing more of her arm against his. "Bet you were a momma's boy." She grinned up at him.

He gave her a shit-eating grin back. "One hundred percent." He nodded.

"So not always a dick then?" Kara shot back.

Derrick barked a laugh. "Nah, not always, I guess. How am I doing now? Falling for my charm yet?"

Kara rolled her eyes with a smirk. "Keep dreaming, Fabio," she joked and knocked her shoulder against his. "Thank you, though."

He nodded. "Anytime, Princess," he said, purposely using the nickname that Johnny had given her.

Kara rolled her eyes. "What's with your crew calling me Princess?"

Derrick laughed. "Oh, come on, you don't see it? Miss CEO up on the top floor of her tower, lording over all the common folk?" He smirked and bumped their shoulders again.

Kara shook her head but didn't disagree. She pulled out her phone and typed in the code, which Derrick committed to memory, and read her notifications. She sighed and slid off her perch of boxes. "I guess break time is over. I've got a meeting in twenty minutes." He watched her open her camera and turn it on herself to use as a mirror. She swiped under her eyes again. Her makeup was still flawless, though her cheeks were a little splotchy. She frowned regardless.

Derrick watched her sigh and tuck the phone into the pocket of her suit coat. She smoothed out her dress and glanced at him. "Thanks for cheering me up. I appreciate it."

He nodded wordlessly. He already missed the warmth of her pressed against his arm.

Once she started walking away, Derrick stood up and followed her. "Have a good day, Princess," Derrick called to her as she opened the door out into the basement hallway.

"Thanks again." She smiled over her shoulder at him.

Derrick smirked as she almost collided with Johnny and Kevin.

"Easy there, Princess." Johnny greeted her with a grin.

Derrick could only imagine how bright red Kara's face grew as she said, "Gentlemen," and squeezed between Kevin and Johnny.

Once the door closed behind them, Johnny raised an eyebrow. "Secret meeting with the queen herself?"

Derrick grinned brightly and glanced at Kevin. "What can I say? She needed an afternoon pick-me-up."

Johnny barked out a laugh, but Kevin glowered. It was too easy to rile the guy up sometimes.

Derrick laughed at his buddy's misfortune.

# Chapter Four

"Sola!" Kara's excited voice jolted Kevin out of his daydreaming. He had been standing in line in the cafeteria, zoned out and waiting to pay for his breakfast sandwich. He looked up from the floor tile he had been staring at just in time to see Kara slide into the back of the woman who was standing in line in front of Kevin waiting to pay for her breakfast.

It was the most *unprofessional* he'd seen her yet: happy and excited but still as put together as usual.

"Morning, beautiful!" Her friend greeted her with a smile. Her hand wrapped around Kara's shoulders in a side hug.

"How'd it go? Did you close?" Kara's smile was bright and genuine. She was so tuned into her friend that she hadn't noticed anyone else in line. Johnny and Derrick stood behind Kevin, also waiting to pay for their food.

"Closed and moved in!" her friend exclaimed. The woman looked older than Kara and was of Hispanic descent.

"Oh my God, Marisol! That's so quick! Congratulations, Sola! That's exciting! What about Jordan? Is he with you or your daughter?"

"Arthur moved in," Erica deadpanned, giving Kara a look.

Kevin watched Kara's eyes widen in shock as her mouth dropped open in a perfect O. *The thoughts that went through his mind as he watched her full lips curve.*

"What the fuck!" Kara exclaimed, then quickly glanced around to see who had heard her. A blush bloomed over her cheeks as she made eye contact with him and noticed Johnny and Derrick behind him.

He smirked but didn't say anything. Johnny and Derrick snickered behind him.

Marisol laughed and nodded as she finished paying and grabbed her food. Kevin moved up in line, set his breakfast sandwich down for the cashier to see, and pulled out his wallet.

"Girl, I asked about Jordan, and you go left field!" Kara cracked, smile on her face, still clearly shocked.

Marisol laughed and nodded again. Both women moved to a counter past the checkout area so they could stand out of the way, but Kevin was still able to hear everything. "Girl, so much has happened!"

"I know! I haven't seen you in two weeks and you've moved in with your ex-husband! Daaaaang girl. Alright we need to do lunch. What's your day look like today? We'll go out." Kara's eyes were bright and excited.

Kevin finished paying but took his time putting his card back in his wallet. He didn't know why he lingered, but he enjoyed seeing her so uncharacteristically unprofessional. He used waiting for Johnny and Derrick to pay as a ruse to hang around.

"I'm open! Noon?" Marisol suggested.

"Yes. Absolutely! I can't wait!" she glanced at her watch. "Shit! I gotta run! I've got a meeting in five minutes. I still need to grab breakfast."

Kevin stepped forward before he even thought about it. "Here," he said, holding out the plastic container holding his fresh-off-the-griddle breakfast sandwich.

Kara turned to him, shock evident on her face. "No, it'll be OK. I'll run back down in a bit."

"It's no big deal. I've got time. Go ahead," he insisted. He could already sense his buddies waiting to give him hell over it.

The blush that spread across her chest and face was breathtaking. "I— thank you, Kevin," she conceded. "I really appreciate this. I'll buy tomorrow. Thank you."

He grinned broadly. "Don't mention it, but I'll hold you to that tomorrow." He winked. He had already given up his breakfast for her, he might as well go the full mile. His buddies were watching after all.

Her blush deepened, but her smile grew wider. "You got it. It's a date." She squeezed his hand before she rushed off.

Once both women were gone, Derrick laughed and shook his head. "Damn bro."

Kevin was too dazed to respond. Instead, he walked back toward the grill to order a new breakfast sandwich.

Derrick was tired of pussyfooting around the subject of Kara. Kevin clearly wanted her. Something had obviously happened between her and Johnny. Derrick could agree there was something special about her. She was hot as fuck too.

Johnny and Kevin had been short with each other ever since "the Breakfast Date," as Derrick was referring to it. Johnny had been more snappish than usual. While Kevin had initially been happy, he was now feeling the rage pouring off their brother.

The three of them sat around a lunch table in the lower-level atrium of the Carmichael building, eating their lunches in silence. They'd been friends and brothers a long time now, from Iraq, to back home to the States, to the brotherhood of the Ravager Knights motorcycle club, an MC formed by Johnny's dad back in the day.

After Iraq, it was the home that Derrick, a.k.a. Devil, had needed.

His brothers in arms.

"It's been a long time since we've shared a chick," Derrick said, being the devil's advocate that earned him his road name. He kept his voice low so only his buddies would be able to hear him.

Johnny snorted and shook his head. "And you think prim and proper Princess is the one to do that with?"

"She's not as prim and proper as you'd think," Kevin answered with a knowing grin.

Derrick chuckled. "'Cause you heard her say *fuck* this morning?" he shook his head. "Nah, I'm with Johnny on this one. No way she'd be into the three of us."

Kevin shrugged, "All I'm saying is she might surprise you."

"Alright, Rockstar," Johnny nodded, using Kevin's road name. "Let's make a bet. First to get in her pants gets to ask if she'd do the three of us." Johnny was dead serious. His blue eyes were stony as he took in his best friend across the table.

Derrick watched as Kevin's whole demeaner changed. He glared at Johnny immediately. "Fuck no. No bet." He shook his head vehemently. "She's not some club whore. She's special, and if you can't see that, stay the fuck away from her," he growled, his dark eyes black as night.

Derrick froze as his friend paused with a fry halfway to his mouth, waiting for Johnny to fly off the handle. He was too used to always getting his way. Vice president of their motorcycle club, second only to his father, owner of Taylor Construction and Mechanical: he was used to giving orders. Taking them? Not so much.

Kevin didn't back down, though. His usual easygoing nature didn't land him in many fights. He and Johnny had been best friends since they were kids. They grew up together in the club. They didn't disagree often, but when they did, it was anyone's guess as to which way it would go.

"You're already in love with her," Johnny stated. He dropped his fry and leaned back in his chair to assess his buddy.

Derrick whipped his gaze back to Kevin. Rockstar didn't deny it. *This* was not how Derrick had expected the conversation to go.

"Son of a bitch." Johnny sighed and shook his head. He ran a hand through his short blond hair, already disheveled from a day of wearing a hard hat.

"Look," Kevin sighed as leaned forward in his chair and rested his forearms on the table, "in the three years I've worked here, we've become friends. She has more in common with us than you think."

Derrick would have laughed if he'd been told that a week ago, but after talking to Kara, however briefly, and learning about her being raised by a single mother, he wondered. She clearly hadn't had the gilded lifestyle that he had imagined, growing up with an über-rich father in some mansion. Meeting a parent as an adult was not easy. And after seeing her break down the other day? It was clear she had a rocky relationship with her father.

"Are you going to claim her?" Johnny asked.

Kevin recoiled, as if he'd been hit. "Fuck no. She's better than this life. Better than all of us." He shook his head. "I wouldn't drag her into our BS."

Derrick glanced at Johnny, who was looking at Kevin almost *cautiously*. Derrick furrowed his brow, once again waiting for Johnny's reaction. "I guess I need to come clean about making a move on her in her office that first day," Johnny admitted.

Kevin's glare was arctic. "What. The. Fuck?" he growled, his voice low.

Johnny nodded, almost looking contrite. "Yeah. After I talked to you, I went back to her office. She had brought back the ice-queen mask, and after seeing her lower her defenses, it was a punch in the gut to see that wall back in place." Johnny sighed and ran a hand over his hair again. He glanced away uncomfortably before he looked back at Rockstar. "I accused her of forcing you into something against your will, and she slapped me."

Derrick's mouth dropped open in shock. A surprised laugh left him before he could stop it.

Kevin wasn't laughing, though. Kevin was raging pissed. Derrick hadn't seen Rockstar that pissed in a while.

Johnny continued before Kevin could speak, though. "She was so fucking sexy man, so I thought I'd rile her up and make her drop the ice-queen bit." He trailed off and shrugged. "I'm sorry, bro. I kissed her. More than kissed her. It was a pretty hot make-out session until she put a stop to it."

Kevin growled low.

"Shit," Derrick muttered, glancing around. Thankfully no one was sitting close enough to hear what was happening.

"Look man, I didn't know how you felt. I wouldn't have done it if I'd known." Johnny put his hands up in surrender. "I just thought you should know what happened. I'll stay away if that's what you want."

Kevin stood up and towered over Johnny, both hands flat on the table as he got in his face. "I'll see you in the ring tonight."

"Alright, brother," Johnny agreed, no questions asked.

Derrick let out a low whistle as Kevin stormed away, anger radiating off him in waves. "I guess that's a no on the sharing," Derrick mumbled under his breath.

Johnny snorted and shook his head.

# Chapter Five

T HE RAVAGER KNIGHTS'S CLUBHOUSE was located on the south side of town in the industrial district, far enough away from residential homes with sound ordinances. It was good planning on their founder's part.

The compound, as they referred to the large lot with multiple buildings on it, included their clubhouse, a sprawling three-story building with multiple dorm-like bedrooms upstairs and a full bar and restaurant downstairs. They served the public, but you had to be a friend of the club to continue to come back.

Also in the compound were the garage where they ran their legit auto-repair shop, a long and sprawling storage shed, half of which they rented out to tenants, and at the back of the lot, the holy grail: the Pit. It was aptly named, for it was originally a fighting pit where the bystanders would stand above to watch the fight take place below.

Over the years, and with a little cash injection, it had transformed into what it was today: an octagonal building that housed a regulation mixed martial arts octagon. The octagon itself was set lower in the middle of the room, with concrete risers surrounding the pit, like stadium seating but there were no chairs, only concrete platforms that raised the crowd above the ring so everyone had a great view no matter where they stood. It was a massive building that held MMA fights twice a year.

Tonight, though, nothing legal was going down.

Devil stood by as both his brothers taped up their knuckles to fight.

A wrong needed to be righted. A respect paid.

Mayhem looked every bit the fighter he was. Thick corded muscles filled out his large frame. His blond hair shone in the bright lights of the Pit. His baby-blue eyes were alight with a crazed fury.

Rockstar lived up to his nickname: a shiny star on a stage, spiky black hair glinting in the lights, his dark eyes narrowed with rage. He was leaner than Mayhem, but every inch of his bare upper torso was corded with muscle. Not an ounce of body fat.

Devil sucked back his cigarette, feeling the buzz of the building. All of their brothers were home for this. The Old Ladies, wives and girlfriends of patched members, were off to the side. They mostly hung together at these events, letting their men hang up front together. Club whores, or *courtesans* as they had been nicknamed for the throwback to the time of knights and courts, walked around in various states of low-cut and super-short, carrying trays of liquor. Hangers-on and friends of the club were also hanging out. A fight night was always a fun night.

The Ravager Knights were hosting guests this evening. Their neighboring charter from Woods Creek was in town for a long weekend. This fight was just the entertainment they were looking for. The fact that Rockstar and Mayhem were using it as a way to settle up between brothers was no skin off their backs.

Ravager Knights President Mac "King" Taylor, Johnny's father, hit the bell three times with a hammer to get everyone's attention. The excitement amped up tenfold.

The crowd pushed forward.

Rockstar and Mayhem took their respective corners.

Devil sucked back his cigarette.

Hotrod climbed into the ring, microphone in hand, his bald head shining in the lights. "Old ladies and gentlemen, bastards and scoundrels," Hotrod called into the mic. A loud roar of hollering answered him. "Whores and courtesans," he paused for the riotous laughter that rose up over the crowd, a wide smile on his face as he looked around. "Brothers from Woods Creek," he continued his grand opening, "we welcome you to the Pit!"

Another loud roar came from the crowd of close to a hundred people.

"Without further ado, I give you our very own Rockstar-rrr and Mayheeemm!" Hotrod dragged out their names as he backed to the edge of the ring.

King rang the bell once and Kevin and Johnny were on each other.

Kevin didn't hesitate. His sucker punch landed right on Johnny's jaw.

Johnny stepped back and shook it off before he grinned. One given shot. One punch to right the disrespect Johnny had shown his brother by kissing his girl. The rest of the fight would be any man's guess. Johnny got in a blow to Kevin's ribs as Kevin punched Johnny's eye.

Derrick leaned against the octagon and rested his arms on the lower rope. He generally loved these fights, but watching his two brothers fighting over something they could be sharing...it didn't sit well with him.

In a slick move, Rockstar ducked Mayhem's punch, got his foot hooked behind Mayhem's and got him flat on his back. He shoved his forearm into Johnny's neck and tossed his legs across too. Just when Derrick thought Johnny might tap out, he managed to flip and reverse the pin on Kevin.

There was a flash of surprise before Kevin grinned and el-bowed Johnny in the ribs.

Johnny grunted, and then they were both on their feet again.

These kinds of fights didn't have any sort of ascertained ending. Not in the case of a brother seeking justice or righting a wrong. The fight could last until they both passed out or their eyes were too swollen to see.

Kevin wasn't the type to hold a grudge, though. Not typically.

Once both men were back on their feet, Kevin grinned and held out both fists for Johnny to knock with his own, a signal that he was willing to forgive and forget.

Johnny grinned and knocked his fists against Kevin's, knuckles hitting. Then they were both hugging in the center of the ring. Hard manly slaps on their backs, but hugging just the same.

Derrick took a deep breath and lit another cigarette. Now that he knew they wouldn't kill each other, he could get a drink. He ignored them both and headed to the bar alone.

If he thought he could get over a little blue-eyed blondie, he'd find some pussy. But he was already so pussy-whipped on her, it wasn't funny. It would just be him and his hand for the evening. Again.

T HE NEXT MORNING, KARA took extra-special care when she got ready. She found a wrap dress that showed a little more cleavage than she generally displayed in the office but was honestly still too fucking conservative by industry standards. It was a deep red color that looked hot on her.

She toyed with the idea of leaving her hair down or at least only putting it up halfway, but she had court and a long twelve-hour day ahead of her. The last thing she wanted to be doing was dealing with her hair.

She headed down to the lower atrium around the same time she did every morning. She glanced around, wondering if Kevin would be waiting and how she might find him if he wasn't. She didn't have to track him down, though. He was waiting in the alcove of the lower-level conference room.

He was wearing blue jeans and a black Taylor Construction T-shirt that fit well, and a black baseball cap was pulled down low over his eyes. She approached slowly, wondering why she suddenly felt nervous. "Good morning," she greeted him with a smile.

"Morning," he murmured. His voice was thick and gravelly.

As she moved closer, she could see his face under the ball cap. His left eye was swollen and bruised. She sucked in a quiet gasp and glanced around. No one around to notice, but you could never be too sure. "Come on," she said, her voice firm. She turned on her heel and left him little choice but to follow her.

She led the way through the lower-level hallways until she walked past the storage room where she'd had her little breakdown with Derrick. She opened the door to the left of it and revealed a dark stairwell lit by dim safety lights.

She flipped a switch to her right and headed down the stairs. Kevin followed without a word. The room below was loud with the noise of a large industrial boiler that helped heat the building. Kara continued down a narrow corridor to a door at the end.

She ushered Kevin into the small abandoned office space that was once used by their facilities manager; he now had an office on the first floor. She flipped on the light and closed the door behind them.

"You're not planning on killing me, are you?" Kevin joked once he turned to face her.

A smile graced her face as she rolled her eyes. She ignored him and reached out to remove his hat slowly. A frown tugged her lips down as she took in his swollen and bruised eye. "What happened?" she asked. She cupped the side of his face and brushed her thumb over his bruise gently.

He slid his hands around her waist and pulled her closer. "Just brothers being brothers," he evaded. His deep voice sent shivers down her spine. The basement was cool, and she was wearing a thin dress. She pressed against his rock-hard body and slid her hands around his neck.

"Damn, you're beautiful," he murmured and pulled her tighter against him.

She blushed and smiled up at him, grateful for the heels that brought her a little closer to him. "That's all you're gonna give me? Some line about brothers being brothers?"

"I'd rather give you something else." He pressed a kiss to her lips before she could ask anything else.

She gasped, and he took advantage and slipped his tongue between her lips. She moaned and closed her eyes while pulling him closer. His hand slid up her back and cupped the nape of her neck, holding her against him. He took charge of the kiss, angling her head and kissing her deeply.

She slid her fingers through the hair at his nape and pressed closer. His kiss was breathtaking, his lips soft and full. He growled and slid his hands down her sides, hands grazing her breasts before they gripped her hips and lifted her like she weighed nothing.

She wrapped her legs around his waist without a second thought, grateful that she had thought to wear a dress with a loose skirt that day.

She gasped when he pressed her back against the cold metal door to the office. She broke the kiss and panted. He kissed his way down her jaw until he reached her neck, where he placed a series of open-mouthed kisses until he bit down gently.

"Fuck," she groaned and arched against him. Her nipples were hard pebbles under her dress. She ground her hips against his and he groaned. He leaned into her and pressed more of his weight against her.

She pulled his hair, maneuvering his head back up. He reclaimed her mouth as one of his hands slid from her hip down her thigh. She moaned into his mouth when his warm fingers slid under her dress. His thumb found her clit through her lace panties, and she moaned again.

It had been so long since she'd gotten laid.

She broke the kiss gasping, and he immediately kissed down her jaw. His thumb pulled away so he could shove her panties to the side. One long, thick finger slid inside her, and she groaned. It had been *way too long*. His finger swirled around once, then twice before he pulled it out and slid a second one in with the first.

She moaned and arched against him.

"You're so fucking wet for me," he growled in her ear, his breath hot on her skin.

She whimpered as he pulled his fingers out partway and curled them forward. His thumb pressed on her clit and started circling as his two fingers hit her G-spot.

She came hard and fast, her orgasm rushing through her. He claimed her mouth mid-yell, silencing her cries. Her body shook as he rubbed her through her orgasm.

"So fucking beautiful," he groaned against her lips, breaking the kiss.

She whimpered when he pulled his digits away.

He sucked her juices from his fingers. "You taste amazing. So sweet."

"Kevin," she whimpered. Her hands slid down his chest to fist in his shirt. "More."

He kissed her again. "I want to do this right," he muttered against her lips. "Have dinner with me."

She whined again. "Yes, God yes," she panted. "But you already bought me breakfast. I don't want to wait any longer."

He chuckled against her lips. "So impatient. You're too used to getting everything your way." He kissed her again before she could respond. "Have dinner with me tonight," he said, his dark eyes alight with desire.

"I have court this afternoon. I don't know when we'll get out."

He nipped her jaw, "So you'll have something to look forward to. Call me when you get out. We can go out, or I can pick something up and we can stay in."

"Stay in, yes, stay in," she moaned.

He laughed and pulled back. He carefully let her down, and she sighed at the loss of his warm body. He pulled out his cell phone and, after he unlocked it, handed it to her. She grabbed it quickly and opened a new text message. She put in her phone number and then texted herself with her address as the message and hit send so she would have his number.

"I'll see you tonight, beautiful." He pressed a chaste kiss to her lips before he pulled away.

Kevin got ready in his room at Johnny's house. Johnny had inherited his grandmother's place after her death. It was located just north of the industrial district, across the Evermore River, a quick ten-minute drive to the clubhouse and set in an older unincorporated part of Mourningside. It had been perfect for the three of them.

By the time Kevin, Johnny, and Derrick had left the Marines, they were so used to shacking up together that Johnny had invited them to move in. That had been five years ago; they never left, and Johnny never asked them to.

Kevin kept his look casual and clean for his date with Kara: dark wash blue jeans and a plain black T-shirt. He was off work, so he slipped on his Ravager Knights cut with its menacing skeleton in knight's armor holding a scythe. The top rocker read "Ravager Knights"; the bottom rocker read "Mourningside" for the city they lived in.

The front of his cut had the United Psychos patch on his right peck that Johnny and Derrick also wore. It was something they called themselves during the Marines that carried over into the club. On his left peck were two rectangular patches stacked on top of each other: "Ravager Knights" and "Death's Henchmen." The Ravager Knights were Death's henchmen to deliver your soul to Death himself.

Kevin may work a day job, but the club came first, *always*. And he was not afraid to get dirty if he had to.

"Whoa, look at you, Rockstar," Devil drawled with a grin as Kevin walked into the living room. Devil and Johnny were sitting on the couch, still in their work clothes from the day. "All showered and looking real purdy. Where you headed?"

Kara had texted Kevin around four that she was leaving court and heading home. She told him to come by around six and said she would cook dinner. "Date with Kara," he announced, locking eyes with Johnny as he said it.

Devil whistled low.

Johnny raised an eyebrow, "You don't think she'll take one look at that cut and slam the door in your face?" He sounded bitter.

"Only one way to find out," Kevin said, knowing full well that this could all blow up in his face. He turned for the door. "Don't wait up," he called over his shoulder. He headed out the back door to the sprawling backyard. The house was set on three acres, and the guys had built a pole barn when they moved in. It housed their bikes and tools, cars, and whatever else they were working on at the time.

The overhead door was still open when he walked out. He made quick work of mounting his Harley and starting it. Once he had his gloves on and sunglasses in place, he pulled his helmet on and buckled it. He was out of the long driveway a moment later.

Kara's address wasn't that far from them. It only took him twenty minutes to get to her house on the west side of the city in an older subdivision filled with newer cookie-cutter homes.

Kara's was no different. A blue Craftsman with white trim everywhere, it was a fairly modest ranch style home with an attached two-car garage. The simplicity of it had surprised him. He had expected some gigantic two-story house with a three-car garage or something extravagant.

He pulled his bike into the drive and parked in front of the closed garage door. He took his time dismounting while looking around and checking out the neighborhood. It was a quiet, tree-lined street. Most of the neighborhood had new homes on the lots, with a scattering of older smaller homes still holding out.

Kevin set his helmet on his handlebar, made sure his black ball cap was situated, and headed for the front door. He had just knocked when the wooden door swung open and the most breathtaking sight stood before him.

Kara's blond hair was down from her usual fancy updo. Large wavy curls fell to the middle of her back. They still looked damp from her shower, but they were drying into massive curls.

She wore a pair of cutoffs and a red tank top. Her feet were bare.

His mouth dropped open in shock as he took her in. He was utterly speechless and stared in awe. For the first time in the three years that he'd known her, her arms were bare. Her heavily *tattooed* arms were bare. She had two full sleeves of black and red tattoos that led from her shoulders all the way down to her wrists. "Holy fucking shit," he breathed, moving toward her slowly.

When she took a step backward, he stopped dead in his tracks. His eyes flew to her face. She held a hand out, gesturing for him to stop.

She wore her own expression of shock. Her eyes flew back and forth over his chest and cut. "Shit," she murmured, her eyes wide.

Kevin tensed. "Kara," he started, keeping his voice low. "Let me explain." He held his hands out in surrender.

Her eyes snapped to his as she broke out of her daze. "Fucking hell, Kevin," she groaned, crossing her arms over her chest. "You're a fucking Ravager Knight! What's there to explain?"

Kevin's eyes narrowed. He hated when anyone immediately drew conclusions based on the cut. He was used to it, sure, but he had expected better from her. He clenched his teeth together, trying not to say something he would regret. "Kara," he started again, his voice steady. "You know me. You've known me for three years. Let me explain it to you."

Kara's gaze searched his face, her eyes darting back and forth between his. Eventually she sighed and nodded before she turned away from him and walked further into the house.

Kevin sighed and took a moment. He let his shoulders sag and tried to relieve some of the tension that had built up. He took a deep breath and finally closed the front door. He left his heavy boots on and followed Kara into the large open-concept great room.

Kara retreated to the large, all-white kitchen that was on the left side of the open room. A massive island served as both a focal point of the kitchen and a demarcation line between the kitchen and living room. Four padded barstools lined the island, giving it a more sophisticated look. The rest of the room was done in shades of tans and browns, with pops of turquoise in the lamps, throw pillows, blankets, and rugs.

It was warm and welcoming and somehow very Kara. At least, the Kara she presented at the office, not this cutoffs-and-tattooed version of Kara that was in front of him. It was a startling contrast and made him realize just how *little* he knew her despite working together for three years.

Kara was stirring something on the stove, and Kevin noticed the smell for the first time. Garlic and oregano. It smelled divine. Kara ignored him as she went to a cabinet to the left of the fridge and pulled out a bottle of what appeared to be whisky. She moved to another cabinet and grabbed two squat snifters.

Kevin stood to the left of the massive island, never feeling more out of place. He watched her move around her home with ease and grace, though he could see the irritation written on her face.

*Goddamn she's beautiful.*

Her fucking hair was amazing, but those damn *tattoos*. He didn't have many himself, only a couple that were covered by clothes, but *damn.*

Black and red ink contrasted against pale skin. There were skulls and butterflies, buildings and gravestones, roses and tulips. Both red and black ink dripped off of pictures and bled into other scenes, making the tattoos look like scenes were bleeding or the ink was running. In any open spaces there were butterflies and stars. There were words scattered throughout, single words float-ing between images: *Dream, Live, Fight.* All randomly located, it seemed, throughout the sleeves except for the words *Live, fuck, die.*

They were grouped together with commas in bright red ink, tatted right under the crook of her elbow on her right forearm, so they'd stand out. On her left forearm in the same location was the phrase *Live in the moment*. Like a reminder to herself. On her right bicep there was a large and menacing skull with red eyes. Kevin eyed the skull, wondering where he had seen it before. There was something familiar about it.

"Now I can see why you wear long sleeves all year, even when it's ninety degrees," he tried to joke. "I just thought it was because the office was freezing."

"Why do think the office is kept freezing?" she deadpanned. She poured two glasses of whisky and slid one toward him.

He glanced at the label on the bottle. Macallan. *Hot damn*. He took a sip of the amber liquid and swallowed slowly. It was smooth going down. Really smooth.

He set down his glass and moved toward her. She was preoccupied with putting the cap back on the bottle. He moved around the side of the island and slid up next to her. "Babe," he murmured. He snaked a hand between her and the counter and rested it on her stomach. He gently turned her to face him. He put both hands on her hips as he towered over her. She was so small compared to him. He was used to her in six-inch heels.

She gasped when she realized just how caged in she was. "Kevin," she groaned and shook her head. Her hand came up and rested on his stomach, between the two open halves of his cut.

He gripped her hips and lifted her onto the island, stepping between her spread legs before she could push him away. He rested his forehead against hers. "Talk to me," he murmured.

Kara felt warm all over. Sitting on her granite counter, caged in by Kevin, his body pressed against hers, she itched to reach out and pull him in for a kiss. She was dying to grab him by the cut and pull him in even closer. He smelled freshly showered, a mix of mint and leather.

Her heart was beating a million miles a minute. Her stomach fluttered at the anticipation building within her. But her lawyer brain was screaming, all the reasons why she shouldn't want this parading through her brain, stomping on her feelings of lust and desire.

She was used to heartbreak in her life. She was used to things being difficult. She had fought tooth and nail to get to be where she was in life. Against all the odds of her childhood upbringing on the south side, with all the disadvantages against her, she'd still managed to make it to the top.

She really didn't want to lose that.

Kara sighed. "You're not going to like what I have to say." She kept her eyes closed; she couldn't look at him. She couldn't see the disappointment on his face. He'd come to mean too much to her in the last three years. Their playful banter and back and forth teasing, seeing his face in the halls when she was having a bad day: his smile had a way of cheering her up without him even knowing.

Kevin tensed. He lifted his forehead off hers.

She opened her eyes to watch his deep chocolate eyes survey her face. He took in every inch of her, as if memorizing her. The longer he assessed her, the more uncomfortable she became. She wasn't used to not being the strongest person in a room. She was a formidable lawyer and damn good at her job. It was her job to make people uncomfortable with just one look.

Being on the other side of the microscope didn't normally bother her because she always knew what her opponent would find. Tonight though, with Kevin? She had a feeling he would see right through her.

She had a feeling she was on the edge of a precipice, choosing whether to take that jump and fall and change everything or to back away and stay safe. It was a pivotal moment with consequences that could either make or break her.

"Say it." Kevin's voice was deep and rough as gravel. His usual warm eyes were hard and almost black, his face a cold mask of indifference.

Kara stifled a gasp at the change in him. He was bracing for the worst.

"I can't." Her voice cracked and she looked away, anger swirling in her belly.

"That's bullshit," Kevin growled. "You don't get to be a fucking coward about this."

Kara's eyes snapped back to his and narrowed. "I'm not being a fucking coward," she spat. "You don't get it, Kevin. I'm the fucking *managing partner* of Carmichael and Associates. The whole fucking city looks to my firm, looks to *me*, to see if I'm gonna fail."

He sneered and stepped back from her. "So, if it doesn't fit into the perfect little image you've crafted for yourself, it's not worth it? That it?" He pressed, his voice rising. "What happened to the girl who covered herself in tattoos?" He grabbed her forearm and held it up. His grip was firm but gentle as he manhandled her.

Kara growled.

He didn't give her a chance to speak. "Live, fuck, die?" he quoted the words dripping in blood-red ink on her arm, tatted on her right inner elbow. "Or these words," he added, grabbing her left arm, "Live in the moment?" He dropped her arms with a scoff and stepped away from her.

She slid off the counter and growled at him. "It's not that fuckin' easy, Kevin," she shot back. "I'm not that same eighteen-year-old kid anymore. Life is not so cut and dr—"

"No, it's not," he interrupted. "It's shades of gray. It's messy. It's real. Or have you forgotten that up in your ivory tower every day?"

"Goddamn it, Kevin," she growled, stomping her bare feet on the floor as she moved toward him. "I fucking know that! It's the only reason you're even standing in my house right now and I didn't slam the door in your fucking face," she shot back.

He stared her down, not moving. His chest rose and fell in rapid succession. His nostrils flared as his jaw clenched. He waited.

"This would be so much easier if I didn't already have feelings for you." She groaned, closing her eyes. She slid her hands into her curls, tugged at her roots, and tried to focus.

He stomped toward her in two strides, his heavy boots slapping on the hardwood floor.

Her eyes snapped open when his callused hands gripped both sides of her face. He angled her head up and leaned down to claim her mouth in a passionate kiss. She melted into him immediately, opening to him. Her hands gripped the two halves of his cut and pulled him tighter against her.

He didn't give her time to object. His hands slid down her body and grazed over her breasts. He gave them not-so-gentle squeezes before he slid his hands to her hips and picked her up. He set her easily on the granite countertop of the island and immediately went for the button on her jean shorts.

She helped him get them over her hips and off before she went to work on his belt and his jeans. She reached into his boxers, wrapped her fingers around his cock, and gasped. She broke the kiss to look down at his thick cock. Her fingers couldn't touch as she wrapped them around his girth.

He groaned and broke the kiss panting.

She slid her hand down his length, marveling at the smooth and warm skin.

He kissed down her jaw to her neck as he pushed her panties to the side and slid a finger home. "So wet for me," he groaned into her ear, his breath hot against her skin.

She pushed his pants down and wrapped her legs around his waist, using the heel of her foot to push him forward. She grabbed his length and guided him to her core. He pulled his finger out of her, sliding it over her clit.

She groaned and he slid the head of his cock through her folds, hitting her clit before sliding back down toward her opening. He slid past her folds and she gasped. He captured her lower lip between his teeth, sucking it into his mouth.

She cried out as he snapped his hips forward and slid home. He was so large, so much larger than she'd ever had before. She wasn't going to last. "Goddamn." He groaned against her lips. "You feel fucking fantastic."

She panted and arched her back against him, angling her hips upward. Her clit rubbed against him, creating the friction she needed.

He pulled down her tank top and bra, pushing her breasts up. His fingers pinched one nipple while his mouth latched onto the other. His mouth was hot and his teeth unforgiving as they clamped down.

Her orgasm crashed over her and she cried out, fingernails digging into his shoulders. He groaned and picked up his pace, riding her through her orgasm. He pulled off her nipple with a loud pop before he captured her mouth again in a bruising kiss.

He groaned into her mouth as he came, hips stuttering against hers.

When he finally stilled and they broke apart, breathless, he rested his forehead against hers and rubbed her cheek while staring into her eyes. It felt like he was seeing into her soul. His dark eyes were so deep and beautiful. He looked right through her. "So, what's for dinner?" he asked after a moment of silence.

A laugh bubbled out of her and set him off. His deep laugh rumbled through her chest, and his wide smile lit his brown eyes from within. He was beautiful. Her heart ached at the thought of letting him go, of seeing him around her office building and not sharing in their usual banter or trading smiles in passing. She had grown attached to him in the last three years, and now that she'd finally had him, how would she ever let him go?

"Kevin," she sighed, closing her eyes. "I can't—I don't—how do we do this?" she finally settled on and slowly opened her eyes.

He watched her attentively. His cock pulsed inside her, and she gasped when his hips snapped forward. How was he hard again already? "I'd say it's pretty easy," he reasoned. He swiveled his hips and drew a long groan from her. "I can continue to fuck you, then we can eat some of this delicious dinner you made for me," he smirked and snapped his hips harder.

She gasped and clung to him. "Don't stop."

"Then, after we eat," he continued, not missing a beat, "we can move this into your bedroom for dessert."

Kara gasped. She could only nod in answer.

He circled her clit with his thumb. "There's a good girl," he responded into her hair.

She moaned and arched against him. He kept his pace steady as he stared down at her.

"Now be a good girl and come for me," he commanded.

Her eyes snapped shut and she shuddered against him. His lips found hers, and he groaned as he came with her, both of them gasping for air.

She could feel his cum leaking out of her. Her thighs were a mess. She was sure there was a puddle of his cum mixed with her juices on the counter beneath her. She didn't care. She felt boneless and weightless, her mind blessedly empty.

He pulled out and grabbed a couple paper towels from the roll. He cleaned himself up and tucked himself away before he grabbed a few more and got them damp at the sink. He turned to her, making quick work of cleaning her thighs and pussy. He was gentle as he moved the warm paper towels through her sensitive folds.

She sighed and slid backward so he could mop off the counter-top before he tossed the paper towels in the garbage. She slid off the counter onto shaky legs. He smirked down at her and gripped her hips to help steady her.

He pressed a kiss into her hair. "Shall we eat?"

She grinned and nodded.

Kevin couldn't believe his luck. She had feelings for him. *Thank fucking God*, he thought. He knew he was taking a risk showing up to her place in his cut, but the club was a part of him. It was his life. He didn't go anywhere without his cut except his job.

She had every right to be pissed. She had every right to throw him out.

He didn't want secrets between them, though. Johnny had been right about Kevin loving her already. He did. In the three years that they'd known each other, he had already fallen for her.

The fact that she already had feelings for him was the icing on the cake. He was determined not to let her get away.

When they sat down to eat their dinner, he pulled her into his lap. He didn't want her to get any distance tonight. He thought if he could keep her close, keep her in a state of bliss and from thinking too hard, he could cement his place by her side.

She snuggled into him immediately, legs curled up against him as she held her bowl of spaghetti against her chest. He had a harder time reaching his food around the bundle on his lap, but he didn't care. He would starve if it meant never letting her go.

"If we're going for full disclosure tonight," Kara started, her fork circling her bowl, playing with her food. "I need to confess something."

Kevin looked down at her. Her blond hair was in disarray. Those goddamn curls would be the death of him. Her face was clean of makeup, her cheeks rosy from exertion. A blush crept up her neck. She stared down at her bowl, refusing to meet his gaze with those shining baby-blue eyes. "Oh yeah?" he asked, keeping his voice even.

"Yeah," she sighed softly. "I uh. Well..."

He'd never seen her so speechless before. The calm, cool, and collected lawyer was stuttering tonight more than he'd ever seen her. "You made out with Johnny," he filled in for her, cutting straight to the chase and easing her burden.

Her eyes snapped to his and she nodded. "Yes. It was weeks ago. When he came to present the plans and have me sign the contract."

Kevin leaned back in his seat and let her talk.

She unfolded her legs and made to get off his lap. He snaked his arms around her hips and held her against him. "I didn't mean for it to happen. I'm not usually so easily provoked. He set me off and

I don't—I'm sorry," she rambled, staring at his chest, unable to meet his gaze. "I'm not usually—I don't do things like that."

He chuckled softly. Her eyes snapped back to his. "Shhh," he murmured and leaned forward. He pressed a kiss to her lips to silence her ramblings. "Johnny has a way with people." He chuckled. "Don't worry. He already told me."

She frowned. A wrinkle formed between her eyebrows. A fire lit in her blue eyes. "He did?"

Kevin nodded, an amused smile on his lips.

"Did he also mention the fact that he said he would go get you and ask you to join us? That you guys shared everything?" Her eyes were bright with an emotion Kevin couldn't place. There was an irritation that bordered on anger, or maybe *desire*?

Kevin took his time watching her. "Did you like that idea?" he asked slowly. He kept his voice low so as not to spook her.

The blush that hit her cheeks was instantaneous. Her mouth dropped open in shock and quickly closed again. He was loving every moment of this evening. If he could spend the rest of his life making her speechless, he would die a very happy man.

Her nod was slow and tentative.

Kevin growled and captured her lips in a biting kiss that was more teeth than lips. She groaned and melted into him. When they broke apart, breathless, she asked. "Is that something you do often? Share women with Johnny?" Her voice was soft and tentative.

He shook his head. "Not often. We have many times, yes," he nodded. "Derrick, Johnny, and I were in the same unit in the Marines," he explained. "It's been the three of us for the last decade at least. They're my brothers. We live together, we ride together, we sometimes share the occasional woman together," he elaborated.

"Derrick too?" she breathed, her eyes clouding over.

Kevin nodded slowly, watching her for any signs of distress.

"I—" she shifted in his lap and turned so she straddled him. "Is that something you would want for us?" Her eyes were so bright and earnest when she looked up at him.

"I'm not going to lie and say I've never thought about it. About how we would make you scream and come undone between the three of us," Kevin smirked.

Her mouth dropped open to form the perfect little O with her plump lips. Her eyes dilated, and she shifted unconsciously in his lap.

"While I've thought about it, that doesn't mean it has to happen. I don't want to lose you," he admitted. "If you want to keep this just me and you, that's all I need, baby."

"But you'd like that?" she asked slowly.

He nodded carefully. He didn't want to spook her, but he wanted all the cards on the table. Full disclosure.

She toyed with the zipper on his cut. Her fingers traced it up and down. He could see the thoughts plaguing her mind. He stayed quiet and let her straighten them out. "I've never done anything like that before." She blushed. "What would that look like? Just sex? Or a full-on relationship?" she asked. She couldn't meet his gaze, but he didn't mind.

A smile tugged at his lips. He was glad she was asking questions. She was fucking smart that way. "I think that's something we'd all have to discuss, together, when the time is right," he answered. He lifted a hand and cupped the side of her face. He used his thumb to tilt her chin up. The blush staining her cheeks was turning him on. His cock was rock hard. He couldn't take much more of this conversation.

"I'm not saying no," she rushed out. "I'm not sure I'm ready for something like that right away..." she trailed off and finally dragged her gaze to meet his.

He captured her lips in a fiery kiss, and she met his intensity. He stood up with her in his arms, and she immediately wrapped her legs around his waist. "Bedroom?" he broke the kiss to ask.

"End of the hall," she panted and reclaimed his lips.

He strode off with her in his arms, ready to settle in for the evening.

# Chapter Seven

JOHNNY GROANED AS HE slid behind the wheel of his F-250 and cranked the engine. He hated driving a vehicle—it felt like he was surrounded by a cage—he'd rather be free, out in the wind, on his Harley. But it wasn't always practical for the day job.

Kevin slid in the passenger seat to his right and immediately rolled down the window. Johnny had the AC cranking, but the truck had been baking in the late May sun all day. It would take a while to cool down.

Derrick grumbled as he slid in the back seat of the crew cab. "Fucking hotter than a witch's tit," he grumbled.

"You sticking around tonight or heading to the Ice Queen's palace?" Johnny asked, shooting a look at Rockstar. Ever since he'd spent the night at Kara's place earlier that week, he'd been alternating his time between the clubhouse and her house.

Kevin slid on a pair of sunglasses. "I'll probably head by hers after the vote." He shot Johnny a shit-eating grin.

Johnny felt his irritation rising. Between his buddy hooking up with the Ice Queen and the *goddamn vote*, Johnny's irritation was through the roof. He needed to get laid. He needed a beer, a joint, and some pussy to relax his mind, body, and soul.

Or at least distract him from the week that never ended.

Johnny shelved his irritation and backed out of the parking spot. He maneuvered the truck around and shifted to drive, heading for the exit of the Carmichael building's main lot, when Devil whistled from the back seat. "Is that who I think it is?" he asked, leaning forward between Kevin and Johnny.

Johnny couldn't believe his eyes. The red Lincoln MKX was pulled to the side of the lot and jacked up on the rear driver's side. A little blond-haired, blue-eyed bombshell was lifting a spare tire onto the lug bolts, having already removed the bad tire.

Johnny pulled the truck to a stop, and Kevin immediately jumped out. "Well hot damn," Devil crooned before he too exited the vehicle.

Johnny rolled his eyes and threw the truck into park behind the Ice Queen's SUV. He took his time getting out of the truck and let the door slam shut behind him.

Kara stood up as they approached.

Johnny could see the exhaustion rolling off her. Sweat dripped down her face. The cream-colored silk shirt she wore was long sleeved despite the 90-degree weather, and it clung to her body like a second skin. Dirt and grease stained the material—she hadn't rolled up the sleeves.

Johnny let his eyes roam her figure unabashedly, taking advantage of her single-minded focus on Rockstar. She had removed the usual suit coat she kept on at all times in the office; her curvy figure was on display, and the silk did nothing to hide it: her large breasts and wide hips, fantastic fucking ass, flat stomach, and thick thighs. She was fucking sexy as hell.

"You OK?" Rockstar asked Kara as he moved toward her.

"Better now," she grinned up at him.

Kevin grinned back at her but didn't move closer. They were keeping shit "professional" at work, according to Kevin.

"Well, look at you, Princess," Devil drawled, moving closer. "Bad bitch, taking care of herself. Dirt looks *real* good on you." He gave her a cocky grin.

Kara's mouth parted slightly and a hint of a blush colored her cheeks. Or was it the heat? It was hard to tell.

"You could have called me," Kevin murmured, stepping closer.

"Could have called AAA, too," Johnny snapped, sick of their lovey-dovey bullshit.

Kara's eyes snapped to his, and Kevin's shoulders tightened.

Ever since Rockstar had spent the night at her place earlier in the week, Johnny had agreed to keep things civil with her, to not go out of his way to rile her up. Seeing her and Kevin together, though was *different*.

Johnny didn't know why it bothered him so much. But seeing the usual Ice Queen so happy and dirty had his cock kicking in his pants as he imagined just how *dirty* she was willing to get.

"Why wait for something I can do myself?" she shot at Johnny.

He smirked immediately, flashing teeth. He watched her eyebrow twitch, like she knew she'd just fucked up. "Really? My brother Rockstar here not doing it enough for you? Still gotta do it yourself after?"

Kevin's head fell back on his shoulders in disbelief.

Devil let out a riotous laugh.

Johnny smirked at Kara. Her face reddened. The glare aimed at him was glacial. *God, I love riling her up.*

"No, Kevin doesn't have that problem. He could give you some pointers, though, if you need assistance getting a woman off," she shot back immediately.

"Mayhem." Rockstar shot at him before he could respond. Johnny snapped his gaze to his brother. Kevin shook his head.

Devil laughed maniacally behind them.

Johnny stalked toward her, his thoughts on their first meeting. How fiery she became. "Tell me Princess," he drawled, "do you think of me often, up there in your office, where I bent you over your desk that first time we met?" he insinuated.

She didn't take the bait; instead she stepped back into Kevin's chest. "I don't have to. My office has been thoroughly christened since then." She smirked.

Johnny ground his molars to keep from snapping at her. Kevin's arm looped around and his hand landed on her hip. Johnny marveled at the size of Kevin's hand on her belly. He always had a bit of a size kink. There was something primitive in his brain that enjoyed picking up a woman and tossing her around a bit, folding her in half.

Seeing Kara next to Rockstar only hammered that home. He bet she was a firecracker in the sack too.

Devil stepped in before Kara could say anything else. "Great work, Boss Lady," he smirked and knelt down next to her SUV. "Where'd you learn to change a tire?"

Kara shot Johnny another glare before she pulled away from Kevin and turned to Derrick. "My brother taught me."

"Damn good thing to know." Derrick nodded and started spinning lug nuts back onto the bolts.

"I was almost done." She shrugged, watching Devil.

"We'll just finish this off for you and you can be on your way." Devil smirked up at her. He reached for the tire iron and started wrenching things down.

Johnny watched Kara blush and ground his molars. "We already know you can handle your shit," he stepped in closer, "but you really that much a prima donna that you can't roll up your sleeves and get dirty?"

Kara's eyes narrowed and she frowned slightly. "It's silk, completely breathable. And dirty. It'll have to be dry-cleaned now."

Johnny barked a sardonic laugh. "Oh no, your poor silk shirt will need to be dry-cleaned." He mocked, still stalking closer.

Her back was pressed against Rockstar's front, the top of her head just below his shoulder. She had to crane her neck to look up at Johnny.

Johnny shot a glance over her head at Kevin. Kevin raised an eyebrow and gave the smallest of nods. Had Johnny not known the man for decades, he might have missed it. Johnny gave him a sharklike grin and stood toe to toe with Kara.

"You're an asshole," she snapped, rolling her eyes. "You're just jealous because I told you no."

He pressed in closer, invading her space. They were practically chest to chest. He could lean forward and press her against Kevin, using his body if he wanted. *Sandwich her between us. That sounds like a good idea.* Her eyes widened as he leaned down to put his face in front of hers. "Funny," he smirked, "that's not how I remember it, Princess."

"I'm all finished here," Devil said, breaking up the tension.

Johnny continued to smirk down at her. She swallowed thickly. *Interesting,* he thought, *did Rockstar have a little conversation with her already?* "Well, Princess," he nodded toward Devil, "that's our cue. Have a nice night." He turned and headed toward the truck.

"I'm getting used to watching you walk away," Kara shot back at him.

"The fuck you say?" he snarled before he even realized it. He spun on his heel, about to march back toward her.

He vaguely heard Devil curse.

"You heard me," she snapped back, crossing her arms over her chest.

His phone rang; he hit ignore without looking at it and stalked toward her in three powerful strides. She held her ground, arms crossed over her chest as she stared him down. Johnny spared Kevin half a glance and saw his brother watching him, amused.

Johnny stepped right into Kara's space. He grabbed her jaw and tilted her head back. She was leaning back against Kevin while he had his hands on her hips. Her eyes widened in shock as Johnny gripped her chin, not so gently, and moved his face toward hers. "Let's get one thing straight here, *Princess*," he drawled. "You may be with my brother now," he grinned wickedly, "but my brother and I *share everything*. And I don't like my women talking back to me," he growled.

She let out a scoff of annoyance. "You fucking asshole," she snapped and pushed his hand away from her face.

Johnny chuckled darkly and grabbed her face again. "Baby, you have no idea," he growled before he slammed his lips down on hers.

"Shit," Devil cursed from behind him.

Johnny's phone started ringing again, and he groaned as Kara's mouth opened to him. He ignored the phone for a moment longer before he broke away breathless. He watched Kara's eyes slowly open as he pulled back and answered the phone. "What?" he snapped.

"Mayhem, it's your dad. Feds just arrested him," Hotrod's voice was clear on the line.

"Motherfucker," he spat, clenching the phone tight. "I'll be right there." He ended the call. "Let's go," he snapped to Rockstar and Devil. Both men were instantly alert, they knew he'd fill them in on the way.

Kevin turned Kara and pressed a quick kiss to her lips. "I'll call you later," he said before he walked past her.

Kara looked shocked and confused, but Johnny didn't have time to think about her feelings right then. He had to leave. He turned on his heel and walked away from Kara without a look back.

Johnny headed toward the truck, barely hearing Devil tell Kara that her wheel was all set, that she just needed to put the hubcap back on, before he climbed behind the wheel of the truck and fired up the engine.

Kevin's and Derrick's doors had barely slammed shut before Johnny was gunning it out of the parking lot, tires screeching on pavement.

It took twenty minutes to get from the Carmichael building downtown to the clubhouse on the south side. Twenty minutes too long for Johnny's temper. "Fucking move!" he shouted as he flew around a car going the speed limit.

Johnny didn't know what he expected to find when they got to the clubhouse. Hotrod had made it clear that his father, was already gone. The feds had been quick about serving the arrest warrant.

It didn't stop him from tearing through traffic and sliding through the open gates of the compound. "Why the fuck are the gates open?" he growled as he parked the truck.

Rockstar shot out of the passenger seat and headed toward the gates. "Close the gates!" he yelled as he walked away.

Johnny climbed out of the truck and stormed into the clubhouse. The main barroom was packed with patrons in for an after-work drink; friends, family, and trusted employees of Taylor Construction loitered around. All of them looked a little rattled in the aftermath of the president's arrest.

"Mayhem!" Hotrod called from across the busy barroom.

Johnny barely spared him a glance. "Church!" Johnny barked to anyone that was anybody, trusting Hotrod and Devil, who was hot on Johnny's heels, would get the word out. Devil peeled off, hearing the demand.

Johnny headed for the double doors at the back of the long room. The bar ran the length of the long wall on the right, some forty feet of counter. Johnny stormed past it and the pool tables and dartboards on the way. He threw the black double doors open and walked around the large conference table that took up most of the room.

As vice president of the Ravager Knights motorcycle club, Johnny's usual seat was at the right hand of his father, the president, who sat at the head. Johnny eyed the seats and slowed his roll as he walked toward them. There was a weight that came with sitting in the top seat. It wasn't his first time filling in for his father over the three years he'd been vice president. There was just something about *this time* that didn't feel right.

He didn't have long to make up his mind, though. Boots scuffed the floor behind him. He took the seat at the head of the table. His brothers filed in and circled around the table to their usual spots. Mammoth, Hotrod, Vagabond, Welder, Bandit, Darrel, and Lemmy sat down. Rockstar and Devil were the last to file in and closed the double doors behind them.

Rockstar took the chair to Johnny's right, not hesitating to take Johnny's usual chair. As club sergeant at arms, the club enforcer, Devil took the seat to Johnny's left. Derrick was one of two club enforcers, along with Welder; their job was to do the dirty work. They were usually called in to torture and end lives.

Welder was in his mid-thirties, with a deadeye stare that could burn through your soul. He may have looked like Mr. Clean with his bald head and bulging muscles, but that's where the similarities ended. He had a thick gray beard that came down to his chest. Johnny couldn't remember if he'd ever seen the guy smile. He was not a man you wanted to meet in a dark alley.

Devil looked downright gentle compared to Welder. Derrick had his Fabio mane of brown hair and a beard that was thick and maintained, about an inch off his face. He looked more hipster, with his long hair back in a ponytail, than club enforcer, but Devil had a switch; once it was flipped, there was no going back. If the Devil came out to play, blood was spilled and lives were lost.

"Alright, what do we know?" Johnny got right to business.

"Not much," Hotrod answered immediately. "Feds tossed this warrant," Hotrod slid a piece of paper at Johnny, "at the bar and said King was under arrest for racketeering, embezzlement, money laundering, and fraud."

"Jesus," Johnny cursed, reading over the arrest warrant, a single piece of paper from the Mourningside FBI branch. It didn't say much. He passed the paper to Kevin when he was finished with it. "And what did they say when they were here? My dad?"

"Your dad denied the accusations, but he didn't say much. Neither did the feds," Mammoth, a behemoth of a man, answered with a gruff sort of growl.

"These are some pretty serious charges." Kevin sighed from Johnny's right. "Has anyone reached out to Danvers?"

"I called him after I called you," Hotrod answered, tipping his head toward Johnny. "He said he would head toward the FBI offices downtown and see what he could find out."

"So we know nothing and have nothing," Johnny snapped.

Kevin sighed and ran a hand through his short black hair. "The warrant mentions Case Holdings LLC. Does your dad have another business we don't know about?"

Johnny snatched the warrant back and reread it. Case Holdings LLC was listed as his father's company. Johnny had no idea what that even was. Mac had started Taylor Construction and Mechanical fresh out of the Marines. He had handed over the reins of the company about five years ago, stating he was ready for retirement from the business and had his hands full being president of the MC.

Any other business was news to Johnny. "I don't know anything about this." Johnny sighed and ran a hand over his spiky blond hair. He scratched at his jaw, fingers sliding through the blond beard that was due for a trim. He tossed the warrant back on the table and leaned back. "There's nothing we can do until we hear back from Danvers. In the meantime, keep the gates closed. I'm not calling a lockdown, but let's stay close to home and no unnecessary outings," he declared, slamming down the gavel signaling the end of church.

# Chapter Eight

K ARA DIDN'T SEE JOHNNY, Kevin, or Derrick in the days that followed the tire change incident. The foreman was missing several workers as well. Kara assumed the missing employees were members of the Ravager Knights. It made sense from a business standpoint. You can't run a company if your whole crew is also involved in illegal activities.

Something had clearly happened with the club that had drawn Johnny, Kevin, and Derrick away so quickly that day; the phone call had obviously been bad news.

She shook her head for the hundredth time, trying to clear her thoughts. This was exactly why getting into a relationship with Kevin was a bad idea. She hadn't seen him since Tuesday in the parking lot. They spoke on the phone in the evenings, but he didn't say much about what was happening. It was club business, and he didn't want to drag her into it.

She had agreed. They were too new to go all in. She wasn't sure if she ever wanted the whole truth of what the club did. Not with her job as a lawyer. So they spent their evenings on the phone, talking about everything and nothing. He told her about his family. His dad had been in the Marines with Johnny's dad, followed him home after discharge, and never left. He had been the VP until he passed away three years ago from lung cancer.

Kevin's mom was still alive and still very much a part of his life. He usually stopped by her house every once in a while for a Sunday dinner with his brothers, Jack and Logan. Logan was married with two boys ages three and four. Jack was single and living it up in Chicago as some big tech guru. He owned his own company and developed tech for the military.

In return, Kara told him about growing up with a single mother in Creekton, a neighboring community on the southside of Mourningside. Often just referred to as the southside, as it had once been apart of Mourningside before it became its own town—it was a rough neighborhood. Marcos, her older brother, came and went. He was ten years older than Kara and had lived on his own since he was eighteen. He helped out their mom when he could with bills and paid for Kara's private school education.

He had been the only father figure she'd had growing up, and she'd idolized him as a young girl. She had been devastated when he moved out at eighteen. But he'd just been another mouth to feed for their momma, and it made sense for him to go out on his own. Their bond stayed strong, though, and he was never far when she or Momma needed him.

When their mother was killed in a car accident when Kara was in her second year of college, Marcos had swooped in and organized her funeral. They'd kept it small, mostly close friends as they hadn't had a lot of family. Her mother thankfully had a small life insurance policy to cover funeral expenses, but there wasn't much left after. Kara's housing had been taken care of thanks to the school dorms and all the scholarships and grants she had earned in high school.

In the summers, she stayed with her brother until she met her father her junior year in college. She'd already declared a prelaw major and had been accepted to a state law program when her father had called her out of the blue. He said he got her number from the university. Kara and Kevin hadn't gotten much deeper into that subject, though. Her father was a touchy subject for her.

Another thing they hadn't talked about was Johnny's kiss. Kevin never mentioned it, so Kara didn't either, and now it was like an elephant in the room whenever she spoke to him. Or at least, that's how it felt to her. She was hoping she would run into Kevin before she ran into Johnny...or Derrick. She felt like she at least needed to clear the air with Kevin. She felt uneasy about it;

everything was still so new, and Johnny wasn't exactly an easygoing guy.

It was Friday when she finally saw Kevin again. She was on her way back from the cafeteria in the lower-level atrium, headed for the elevators, when he stepped out of his usual alcove of a conference room. She looked up to find him smiling down at her.

His bright grin took her breath away. Butterflies started in her belly, and she felt herself blushing despite talking to him regularly. He looked amazing. His black hair was styled in a messy bedhead fashion. He had a red plaid, short-sleeved button-up shirt on over a white T-shirt. He clearly hadn't planned on working much that day. "Good afternoon, Miss Carmichael." He grinned as he fell into step with her.

"Good afternoon, Kevin." She beamed, happy to see him.

His dark eyes shone as he smiled down at her. "You have some free time this afternoon?" he asked, slowing to a stop where the hallway came to a T, glancing around. They could either follow the hallway further underground toward the loading dock near the back of the building or they could take the T to the elevator bank.

"Yeah, my afternoon is clear. I was thinking of taking off early today." She smiled. It was past two p.m. and she had been thinking of cutting out early.

His smile turned tight. "I, uh, I was hoping for some legal advice actually," he hedged and glanced around again.

Kara frowned slightly. He was acting cagey and she didn't like it.

"Johnny's dad was arrested. We were hoping you could give us some advice, maybe point us in the right direction. We have a lawyer, I just think this might be above his pay grade a bit," Kevin explained.

Kara's frown deepened. "How about this," she started and glanced around just as Johnny and Derrick rounded the corner from the loading docks, "come up to my office and I'll listen, and we'll go from there," she said, speaking mostly to Johnny at that point.

She took in his slightly haggard appearance. He wore a basic black Taylor Construction T-shirt and blue jeans with brown boots, but his blond beard was longer and more unkempt than usual. He had a black ball cap pulled down low, like he was trying to cover his baby-blue eyes, but she could see the dark circles under them.

Johnny nodded at her, and she turned away from him quickly.

"Hello, Princess," Derrick greeted.

"Derrick." She smiled and rolled her eyes as she led the way to the elevators. He too had a black work shirt on and blue jeans with boots, but his long brown hair was loose around his shoulders, a full mane of silky, beautiful hair that begged for her to run her fingers through it. His thick beard was neatly trimmed, and his green eyes were mischievous as he took her in.

She wore clean boot cut blue jeans that hugged her body and a maroon silk shirt that had billowy sleeves. No suit jacket today. She was the most dressed down she got in the office. A pair of six-inch booties completed the look and dressed it up a little more. She also let her hair down a bit. She had straightened her crazy curls and pulled it up halfway, leaving it down in the back. Straightened, it almost reached her ass.

The four rode up together in the elevator. Derrick kept eye fucking her the whole ride up. She eyed him with an amused smirk but mostly ran her eyes over Kevin.

Johnny had kept his eyes straight ahead and his jaw clenched. When the elevator doors opened and she stepped out, she saw Kevin clamp his hand down on Johnny's shoulder, squeezing measuredly. He clearly hadn't been doing well since his father had been arrested, she assumed on Tuesday, when they left in a hurry after that phone call.

They took the chairs in front of her desk, and she pulled out a pad of paper and a pen. When the three men were settled before her, she finally asked Johnny to explain. He leaned forward and rested his elbows on his knees. He cleared his throat and started talking. "FBI picked up my old man Tuesday. The warrant was for racketeering, embezzlement, money laundering, and fraud. The feds say he was embezzling money using a shell company. Case Holdings. Apparently he owns it. I don't know," Johnny shook his head. "He doesn't even know how to work a computer. Not really. Not to be the tech genius he's being accused of being."

Kara felt the blood drain from her face as Johnny spoke. Even her best court mask wasn't enough for the heart-wrenching anxiety that flooded her. Case Holdings. She knew that name. She had seen the records that someone at Carmichael and Associates had been paying them for years.

"Can you gentleman write down your numbers for me please?" Kara asked, grateful that her voice came out strong and not as shaky as she felt, passing around the notepad and pen.

She watched Johnny and Derrick quickly jot down their numbers. Derrick gave her a sexy smirk that would have had her melting had the circumstances not been so dire. Once she had their numbers, she quickly pulled out her own phone and opened a new text message and started a group chat.

"I am so sorry to hear that Mr. Taylor," she spoke louder and more clearly than she usually would in her office, all while typing out a message. "I won't be able to help you, I'm afraid."

Johnny glared at her. "What was the point of even bringing us up here if you weren't going to help?"

She quickly sent the message. ***Meet me at Sullivan's Bar on Bright Street in an hour.***

Derrick caught on before Johnny and pulled out his phone. He quickly read the text and showed it to Johnny. Johnny read it before looking back to Kara with a slight nod.

"I'm so sorry, Mr. Taylor," she said again, standing this time. She glanced at Kevin, who nodded, before she turned back to Johnny.

"Yeah, thanks for nothing." Johnny rolled his eyes and headed toward the door.

"I do hope everything works out for your father," she added as she followed them toward the door.

"Thank you for your time, Miss Carmichael," Kevin said before he followed after Derrick and Johnny.

Kara sighed when they were out of sight and closed her door. Her secretary barely spared her a glance. Kara's heart was racing. Her anxiety was on high. Case Holdings was something she had been looking into as discreetly as she could for the last year.

Even though her father had retired a year ago, he still had many of his minions walking around with their hands in everything, her father's hands in everything. Anytime she felt like she got close to finding out about Case Holdings, files suddenly were moved or corrupted.

She had mentioned the name to her father once over dinner, and he had quickly brushed her off and swept it under the rug. "Oh, don't worry about the miscellaneous accounting. We have some of the best accountants and forensic accountants on the payroll. Let them do their jobs so you don't have to," her father had said.

She had dropped the subject then.

Now it was suddenly popping back up? With an outsider involved—a contracted company that her father had hired personally three years ago? None of it made sense. She couldn't go to her father about it, but she might be able to go to Johnny and maybe his father to learn more. She would find out what was going on one way or another.

Johnny and his brothers rolled up to Sullivan's on their Harleys, in full colors, an hour later to meet Kara. The bar was not quite a dive but not as upscale as he would expect someone like her to frequent. It was also far enough from Carmichael and Associates that they shouldn't have to worry about anyone from there overhearing.

He had been angry when she first told them she couldn't help, but when Derrick had shoved his phone in front of Johnny's face in her office, he was intrigued. There was something going on, and he was going to get to the bottom of it.

They found her already seated at a high-top table in the middle of the semibusy bar.

Johnny stopped when he saw Kara. Her blond hair was up halfway, like she'd it in the office, but the blouse was gone. Instead she wore a black tank top with a skull and bright red roses on it. She had on cutoffs and flip-flops.

"Hot damn," Devil breathed next to him.

"Fuck me," Johnny groaned. Even from a distance he could make out the bright red ink contrasted against the black and her pale creamy skin. Full sleeves never looked so fucking hot.

Kevin laughed and pushed past them, taking the lead toward Kara.

Johnny moved slowly, following. He could only watch as Kara greeted Kevin with a smile before Kevin grabbed her jaw and tilted her head up to meet him in a passionate kiss right in the middle of the bar. Johnny watched her eyes close.

The show of dominance had Johnny stiffening in his jeans immediately. He moved slowly toward the table, watching Kevin with Kara. They were breathtaking together, Kevin's black hair and tan skin against Kara's creamy skin with her blond hair. It was a night-and-day contrast until her heavily black-and-red-tatted arm slid against his. Her hand wrapped around his wrist just as his hand that gripped her jaw flexed.

Kara forcefully pulled away from Kevin, tugging his hand from her jaw as Devil and Johnny came up to the table. She was flushed, and Johnny smirked when she looked his way. "Well, well, well. Not so prim and proper after all?" Johnny drawled and slid onto the barstool next to her.

Kevin chuckled and took the stool to her right, across from Johnny at the small square bar-top table.

Kara rolled her eyes at Johnny and took a sip from her beer. A Miller Lite, not some hoity-toity craft beer. Johnny was actually impressed even if he was more a Bud Light guy.

Devil took the seat across from Kara and crossed his forearms on the table. He leaned on the table toward her and smirked. "Hot damn, baby girl," Devil drawled.

Kara's flush deepened down her neck and chest. The tank top showed a generous amount of cleavage, and Johnny just wanted to lick and bite her exposed skin.

A waitress walked over with a steaming platter of nacho fries that were loaded with four cheeses and bacon. She set the plate down in the middle along with four smaller plates. The waitress swapped out Kara's empty beer for a fresh one and turned to the guys. "Hello gentlemen. My name's Jenny. What can I get for you?"

"Miller Lite," Kevin answered.

"Bud Light," Johnny and Derrick replied.

"You want a few minutes to look over the menu?" she asked.

"Yes, please," Kara nodded and passed out menus.

"Sure thing. I'll be back with your drinks." Jenny smiled before she walked away.

Kara started digging into the loaded fries with a fork and scooped a bunch onto her little plate.

"I figured you'd be more of a salad girl." Johnny smirked.

"That's because you don't know a damn thing about me, Johnathan Taylor," she shot back at him, leveling him with a look.

*Alright, touché*, he thought. *Point taken.* "You're right," he admitted and nodded once.

She took a sip of her fresh beer and turned to Derrick, who had yet to take his eyes off her. Presently, they were settled somewhere on her cleavage. "My eyes are up here," she drawled.

Derrick grinned brightly and snapped his gaze up to her eyes. "And they're beautiful," Derrick answered immediately, "just as beautiful as the rest of you," he smoothly added, waggling his eyebrows comically.

Kara flushed again, though she smiled and rolled her eyes. "Let's order, then we can talk about what's going on," she deflected.

Johnny shrugged and picked up his menu.

Kara dug into the cheesy fries with a vengeance, clearly starving and already knowing what she wanted.

Once Jenny had dropped off their beers and they'd ordered, Johnny prompted Kara. "Why the cloak and dagger?" he asked, getting straight to the point.

"This goes deeper than you know." She leveled a stare at Johnny and continued. "Someone at Carmichael and Associates is using Case Holdings to embezzle money. They have been for a while now."

Johnny let out a frustrated sigh and ran his hand over his head. "Do you know who?"

Kara shook her head. "I've been digging into this for a while now. I haven't made much headway," she admitted. "Have you been able to talk to your father? Has his lawyer met with him?"

Johnny shook his head. "I haven't been able to talk to him. His lawyer met with him yesterday, and Dad didn't say much. Just the charges and that Case Holdings is the company he opened forty years ago. He was going to start a business, but it never panned out, so he never did anything with it. The tax ID and name have just been sitting out there unused this whole time. He thought the registration would have expired decades ago and that was that."

Kara nodded slowly, a frown on her face. "It should have, at least the business license would have. The real question here is, why is it associated with Carmichael and Associates?"

Johnny scratched at his jaw, his nails scraping over the thick beard. "I don't know," he admitted, shaking his head. "My old man didn't give Danvers much to go on, just that he let the company go practically right after he started it."

"Danvers, as in Freddy Danvers?" Kara asked, raising an eyebrow.

"Yeah, you know him?" Kevin asked.

"We've met." Kara nodded thoughtfully, leaning back in her chair and taking a sip of her beer. "The law world is a relatively small one, though I generally stick to corporate law. He's good, though, from what I hear."

"He's been the club's lawyer for several years now." Johnny nodded.

Kara dipped her head and opened her mouth to speak, but Jenny came over with a tray full of food and more beers.

She made quick work of setting everything down and asked if they needed anything else.

When she was gone, Johnny looked over at Kara's plate to see a large bacon cheeseburger on it. He watched her squeeze ketchup on it before she cut it in half. When she raised it to her mouth and took a large bite, her eyes closed and she let out a low moan that immediately had his cock stirring.

"Fucking hell, baby girl," Devil's voice was gravel. He sounded about as rough as Johnny felt.

Even Kevin wasn't immune if his stare was anything to go by.

Kara slowly opened her eyes and giggled softly. "Sorry. I like my meat."

"You just gonna walk right into that one?" Johnny asked her, making Kevin laugh.

"Walked into nothing," she shot back with a grin. "Baited easily."

Johnny growled and hooked his foot around the leg of her barstool and slid her around the table toward him. It was a quick move that had her lurching forward. Her hand landed on his thigh to catch herself from falling to the floor. Her face was inches from his when she looked up at him startled. He didn't give her a second to recover. "I'm not the baitin' kind, Princess," he murmured before he grabbed her jaw and kissed her.

He was nowhere near as rough as he had been in the parking lot or even her office. He kept the kiss chaste, letting her decide how this would go. He didn't have to wait long. Her free hand came up and combed through his unruly beard, holding him to her. Her mouth opened and he followed her lead, allowing her to set the pace as their tongues mingled together.

"Jesus," Derrick groaned.

Johnny kept the kiss short. When he pulled back, Kara was slowly opening her eyes. Her sky blues stared back at his own. Her lips were still slightly parted, and her warm breath puffed against his lips.

# Chapter Nine

KARA WAS IN OVER her head. There was no doubt about that. Johnny's eyes were dark with desire. His kiss had been soft and almost sweet. As sweet as a man like Johnny Taylor could get, she imagined. Reluctantly she pulled away. She looked at Kevin and saw the desire written clear as day on his face. His brown eyes were almost black.

They may not have talked about her last kiss with Johnny, but it was obvious they would be talking about this one.

She looked away only to lock eyes with Derrick. His long brown hair was around his shoulders, and his green eyes had a mischievous glint to them. The usual playful grin was gone. There was an intensity to his gaze that she wasn't used to seeing.

She felt naked as she stared him down. Not used to backing down, she raised an eyebrow at him and reached for her drink. She had a feeling she was seeing a hint of the club enforcer for the first time.

"So what are your thoughts on the case?" Kevin asked, drawing her attention away from Derrick.

She took a sip of her beer before she looked over at Kevin and saw the smile tugging at the corners of his lips, though he tried to hide it. He had told her outright that he shared everything with these two. He didn't seem bothered by their behavior. Kara cleared her throat. "Why don't you text me Danvers's number," she said, looking at Johnny. "Did he say where they were holding your father?"

"You'll help us?" Johnny asked, not answering her question.

"Danvers will still be lead counsel," she corrected. "I'll help Danvers as much as I can. He'll still have to represent your father in court, but I can help dig and gather as much information as I can. Help him prep—"

Johnny cut her off midsentence with another kiss. This time he gripped the back of her neck and her jaw with both hands and pulled her toward him. Her barstool was still next to his, so he didn't have to reach far to manhandle her into the position he wanted. A part of her bristled at being moved so roughly, but her wet panties and clenching pussy said otherwise.

She bit down on his bottom lip and he groaned. She pulled away roughly. "You keep doing that," she grumbled, slightly annoyed.

"Haven't heard you complaining," he shot back, his voice like gravel. His arrogant stare was obnoxious. It was so fucking hot.

She rolled her eyes and pulled away. He let his hands drop from her face. When one landed on her thigh and stayed there, she looked up at Kevin. He had been oddly quiet this whole meal.

He smirked and shoved a fry in his mouth when she met his gaze.

They finished their meal quickly and in relative silence. Johnny kept his hand on her bare thigh and occasionally rubbed circles with his callused fingers. Her stomach was in knots. She didn't know how she managed to finish her meal without shaking.

When she was done, she excused herself to the bathroom and slipped away from the table. She followed the wraparound bar toward the back of the restaurant, where there was a hallway that led to the bathrooms.

Turning the corner, she slid up to the bar, where their waitress was standing. "Hey, can I get you something?" Jenny smiled sweetly.

Kara grinned and slid over her black card. "Can you throw everything on my card? I don't want them to argue."

Jenny grinned brightly. "Sure thing. The whole tab?" she confirmed.

"The whole tab," Kara nodded.

Jenny nodded and walked away to take care of it.

"What do you think you're doing?" a deep voice asked in her right ear at the same time tattooed arms caged her in against the bar. A hard body pressed flush against her back.

Kara jumped slightly when she felt a slight scratch of beard on her neck before an open-mouthed kiss was pressed to the side of her neck. "Derrick," she moaned softly. Her hands came up to brace on the bar. They were tiny compared to his large ones on either side of hers.

He continued to press wet kisses on the column of her neck until he reached her ear, then he sucked her earlobe into his mouth. She whimpered when he bit down slightly. "Derrick," she breathed.

"What are you doing over here, baby girl?" he questioned, though from his tone, it was clear that he knew exactly what she was doing.

"None of your business, Derrick." She groaned when his mouth latched onto the junction of her neck and shoulder and he sucked, hard.

"Try again, baby girl," he muttered.

She pushed back against him, using the bar as leverage to push him off. He stepped back a step, and she whirled around to face him. She quickly realized her mistake when he grinned wickedly and stepped into her, pressing her back against the bar.

His mouth was on hers before she could utter a word. His hands were on her a moment later. One slid up her back and fisted in her hair, holding her head in place. The other was under her shirt at the small of her back, hot on her bare skin. His mouth devoured hers. His lips were soft and malleable against hers. His tongue, hot in her mouth.

He was so much larger than her five-foot-three frame. There was a reason she wore six-inch heels everywhere. But she had run home to change after the office and slipped into flip-flops once she was comfortable. He had to easily be six-four or six-five, and he was broad-shouldered too. He towered over her and crowded her against the bar.

She groaned and pressed her hands against his chest. She was gearing up to push him away, she really was. His mouth worked magic against hers, though. And he still had a fist full of her hair.

"Here's your card back." Jenny spoke up loudly behind Kara.

Kara jumped slightly and pulled away from Derrick as much as he'd allow. She managed to turn in his arms when he finally let go of her hair, grabbed her card, slid it in her back pocket, and quickly signed the receipt. She added a fifty-dollar tip and quickly pushed the paper and pen back toward Jenny.

"Naughty, naughty, baby girl," Derrick murmured in her ear before he turned her back around to face him. His hand wrapped around her jaw and pulled her face up to look at him.

"Because I decided to buy dinner?" Kara rolled her eyes. "Drop the caveman act, Fabio. It ain't cute."

Derrick let out a low growl and picked her up by her hips. She had no choice but to wrap her legs around his waist and her arms around his shoulders as he stepped away from the bar. "I'll give you caveman," he grumbled and walked down the hallway toward the bathroom in the back of the bar.

"Derrick, put me down," she snapped, slapping his shoulder.

"Oh no, baby girl. You've got Devil, now," he growled and slammed open the door to the men's room.

There was a man at a urinal who looked up at the commotion. Derrick paid him no mind and headed toward the handicap stall in the corner. He slammed the door closed behind them and quickly locked it. Then he spun and slammed Kara against the tile wall.

She let out a slight "eep" when her back pressed against the cool tile. Devil quickly covered her mouth with his, and she easily lost herself in him. She closed her eyes, gripped his shoulders, and pulled him tight.

He chuckled under his breath, his chest reverberating against hers. His fingers deftly undid the button and zipper on her jean shorts, then he was pulling away from her. He set her down long enough to rip her jeans and thong down her legs. She moved to reach for his buckle, but he was faster. He undid his belt, button, and zipper in record time. His pants dropped to his knees immediately, and he picked her back up.

She went easily. She found it was easier to let him manhandle her.

He claimed her mouth as he reached down and freed his cock from his boxers. He slid his cock through her folds. "Jesus, baby girl. You're so fucking soaked." He groaned against her mouth.

"Fuck." She moaned when he slid inside her. He took his time, inching in and out, ensuring he was wet before he pulled out and slammed in to the hilt. He swallowed her cries as he kissed her. He was big. As big as Kevin, if not bigger.

His pace was hard and brutal. All she could do was hold on and enjoy the ride. When she broke their kiss, panting, he licked his way down her neck, pausing when she let out a low moan at a sensitive spot. "Fuck Derrick," she groaned as he continued to suck a spot on her neck below her ear.

Her orgasm shattered over her as he bit down. He groaned as she shook against him. Her walls quivered and body undulated. She clenched her teeth to keep from crying out. Instead, she let out a quiet moan, her head tossed back against the wall.

"Fucking hell, baby girl," he panted. He rode her through her orgasm, slowing to let her come down. He groaned when she swiveled her hips. He didn't last much longer after that. She continued to swivel her hips, and he sank his teeth into her neck and groaned. His hips shuddered against hers as he came.

It took them a moment to catch their breath before he pulled back to look at her. There was a devilish smirk on his lips. "Not so prim and proper after all?" he chuckled.

She rolled her eyes. "Guess not, biker boy," she quipped back.

"That's Devil to you, baby girl," he smirked.

Doubt started creeping in, and she frowned slightly. "Derrick, we didn't use a condom," she sighed.

He shook his head immediately. "Don't worry. I got tested. All three of us did when Kevin said he had a date with you. And I always use a condom with the courtesans at the clubhouse."

She wrinkled her nose. "Courtesans? As in whores from back in the day? Like eighteenth century?" she questioned.

He grinned brightly. "Yep. We're knights after all."

She let out a laugh of disbelief. He looked so smug. "Fucking bikers." She shook her head.

"Yeah, baby girl, that's what you're doing. Fucking bikers." He smirked again.

She smiled and groaned at his bad pun. "Alright, Devil. Let me down." She patted his shoulder with her hand.

He slid out of her, both of them groaning, before he put her down on shaky legs. He waited until she was stable before he reached down and did up his boxers and pants.

Kara ignored her underwear and shorts and opted to use the toilet. She peed and then cleaned herself up as much as she could with rough toilet paper. When she was done, Derrick handed her her shorts sans underwear. "Derrick, give me my undies," she said, holding out her hand.

He smirked and pressed a kiss to her lips. "Mine now."

"Derrick," she snapped half-heartedly.

"You don't need them," he grinned devilishly.

Her OCD mind was kicking into gear. "Derrick, they match the bra. They're a set. I'll give you another pair," she reasoned.

His grin grew wicked. "Little miss control freak doesn't like a little chaos in her little orderly world," he goaded. "Put the shorts on, baby girl, or I'll take them too. Consider it your punishment for buying dinner." He turned and opened the stall door with her still standing there half naked.

She gaped after him but had no choice but to slip into the jean shorts. They were snug from the get-go, but now the seam rubbed against her folds and hit her clit, and she gasped as she walked out of the stall.

Derrick was standing by the bathroom door, a devilish grin on his face as he watched her move toward the sinks. "How's that feel?" he asked.

She ignored him and washed her hands. She fixed her hair and made sure her makeup still looked good before she dried her hands and turned back to Derrick. "I will get those panties back," she declared.

He just smirked and held the door open for her.

She rolled her eyes and walked past him. She could feel his eyes on her ass as she walked, and every step sent a jolt through her clit. She felt like everyone in the bar knew what she did in the bathroom with Derrick. She was a mess by the time she reached the table and slid back on her stool.

Kevin shot her a wink, a smile on his face. Either he didn't know what transpired in the bathroom with Derrick or he was OK with it. She needed to talk to him about it. Hopefully tonight.

She hadn't realized how close her stool still was to Johnny's until his hand landed on her thigh. "Have fun in the bathroom?" he asked before his finger slid under the hem of her shorts and rubbed against her slit.

She gasped and froze; her eyes flew to Kevin's. His dark brown eyes were almost black. A smirk tugged at his lips as he leaned forward, crossing his arms and resting them on the table. "Did I neglect you this week, baby?" he asked, his voice low. "I wasn't around much, so you had to fuck my brother in the bathroom?"

She gasped, mouth dropping open as Johnny slipped a finger inside her pussy at the same time. She had no words. Devil chuckled deeply.

"Such a little slut, you need my best friend to finger you right after you got fucked?" Kevin continued.

"Kevin," she moaned and shifted forward on the stool toward him. The angle drove Johnny's finger in deeper, and she let out a shuddering breath and closed her eyes.

"She's dripping and not wearing panties. You let Devil fuck you without a condom?" Johnny's voice was deep and rough. He twisted his wrist and slipped in a second digit.

She panted. She needed to get her head on right. She was in the middle of a semibusy bar. Anyone could be watching. Anyone could see what was happening beneath the table. She was a goddamned lawyer. She needed to get herself under control.

Her eyes snapped open and she glanced around quickly. But no one seemed to be paying them any attention. Kevin and Devil were crowded around the small table and blocked most of the view with their bodies.

"It was her punishment for buying dinner," Derrick told his brothers.

Johnny tsked in her ear. "Is that right, Princess? You buy our dinner?" his wrist twisted again, and then his thumb was on her clit. The two fingers inside her curled upward, and his thumb circled her sensitive bud.

She couldn't respond. Her eyes snapped shut as his fingers circled over her G-spot. She whimpered when they stopped. She opened her eyes to see all three men watching her intently, desire clear on their faces. She gasped. She was not used to having undivided attention during sexual activities. Especially with three guys at once.

She blushed and tried to hide her face in Johnny's shoulder.

Kevin grabbed her hand. "Uh-uh, baby," he shook his head.

Her eyes snapped to his. "If you want to come, you'll answer the question."

"What question?" she asked immediately.

Johnny's laugh rumbled out next to her. "Look at you. Miss calm, cool, and collected, always got an answer for everything, coming undone over a couple fingers in her cunt."

Kara narrowed her eyes at him. He rubbed circles into her G-spot again, and she lost her train of thought. Her eyes closed again, and she bit her bottom lip to keep from moaning.

"Why does it matter if I bought dinner?" She groaned.

"Call us old fashioned." Derrick's amusement was evident in his voice; even with her eyes closed she knew he was smirking.

"Neanderthals, more like it," Kara snapped.

"Princess, if I were a Neanderthal I'd fuck you right on this table in front of everyone," Johnny growled in her ear. "Now, be a good girl and come for me," he ordered.

She buried her face in his shoulder and bit down on the leather of his cut as her orgasm washed over her. She whimpered slightly and squeezed her thighs together as her pussy clenched down on his fingers.

"There's a good girl," Johnny murmured and pressed a kiss to her hair.

Her mind went gloriously blank at the praise and the orgasm, and she felt like she was floating. She leaned further against Johnny as he pulled his fingers from her pussy and wiped them on his jeans. His hand landed on her thigh and squeezed. "You coming to the clubhouse tonight?" he asked, his voice softer than she'd ever heard it before.

She looked to Kevin, unsure of what to do. He smiled at her and said, "Up to you."

"You should come to the clubhouse tonight," Johnny suggested.

She looked up at him, unsure. "This, whatever this is, between the four of us," she spoke slowly, trying to decide on her words. She looked at Kevin and glanced at Derrick before she looked back up at Johnny. "It's just the four of us, right? This won't go further? I'm not some club whore that you'll share with—"

Johnny cut her off before she could continue. "No. You aren't a whore despite what we might have said during the heat of a moment. We would never share you with anyone but the three of us," Johnny growled.

She opened her mouth to ask more, but Derrick cut her off too. "Ours, baby girl," he said. "Just ours," he added.

"Does that make you mine?" she questioned, looking between Derrick and Johnny. She already knew she had Kevin, but was it selfish of her to demand that they only sleep with her?

Johnny pressed a bruising kiss to her lips. "We're yours, baby," he said when they broke apart, breathless.

She looked to Devil, who nodded back at her. She gave him a dazed smile before Kevin cleared his throat. "Shall we get out of here?" he asked, cocking his head.

She nodded slowly.

"I'll follow Kara back to her place so she can drop off her car, and then we'll head over to the clubhouse," Kevin told the other two.

Johnny and Derrick agreed, and they all stood up and left the table. Once outside, Derrick grabbed her wrist and whirled her around. She spun into his arms and gasped when his hand came up and grabbed her jaw. "No panties," he ordered.

Her eyes widened before she glared at him. "You don't order me—"

A hand came down on her ass, the loud smack making her jump before she felt the sting of the hit. "And you don't talk back when given an order," Johnny growled into her ear before he pressed himself to her back and sucked a bruising kiss into her neck.

She whimpered and closed her eyes. How the hell did they find that sensitive spot on her neck so quickly? Johnny's hands were on her hips, Derrick held her face with one large hand while the other slid behind her head and fisted in her hair. His lips were on hers a moment later, and she groaned as he stepped into her body, sandwiching her between him and Johnny.

She was in so much trouble. If this was any indication on how the night would go, she would be thoroughly *fucked* by the end of the night.

"Alright, horndogs," Kevin's voice penetrated the fog that surrounded Kara's brain. "Let her breathe. We're in public."

It was the jolt of reality that Kara needed. She abruptly pulled away from Derrick only to back further into Johnny. She turned and stepped out of his arms as well, quickly looking around to see if anyone had seen them.

She didn't see anyone, but fear set her heart racing. "Relax baby," Kevin said as he stood next to her. "No one saw, but we should get going."

She gave him a nod and headed toward her Lincoln, parked on the street a couple spaces down from the bar.

"I'll meet you at your place." He nodded to her.

She smiled and got into her vehicle.

# Chapter Ten

KEVIN WAITED FOR KARA to drive away before he turned to his two best friends. Both of them watched him, waiting. "We need to do this right," he started. He could see Johnny's hackles rising already. His buddy didn't like being told what to do. "I don't want to lose her," he added.

Johnny blew out a breath and nodded. "Alright."

"I think she's on board," Derrick said and rubbed a hand over his beard thoughtfully. "We should discuss limits though. It's clear she's into some of the power play dynamics. Definitely saw that praise kink for what it was. You already talked to her about the three of us sharing, then?"

Kevin nodded and ran a hand over his black hair. "She's never done anything like this before, obviously, but she's not opposed. She said she wasn't ready a couple weeks ago." He shrugged.

Derrick laughed. "Well, she seems ready now."

Kevin nodded and grinned before he looked at Johnny. "And if she changes her mind when she gets to the clubhouse?" Kevin asked him, already knowing his brother's response.

"Well then she says no and goes about her night." He shrugged.

Kevin nodded again. "Alright, I'll see ya in a bit," he said and turned toward his bike.

Kevin made it to Kara's house relatively quickly. He let himself in her front door without knocking and went in search of her. He found her in her bedroom packing a small bag. She looked up when he walked in. "I assume I'm probably not coming home tonight?" she asked.

He grinned brightly. "Only if you want to," he said, then moved into her space. He turned serious for a moment. "Kara, nothing has to happen tonight if you don't want it to. Just say the word. At any point if you want to stop, if you want to leave? Just tell us, and we won't get upset. I promise," he said as he wrapped his arms around her waist and pulled her against him.

She smiled softly and leaned up on her tippy-toes to kiss his lips. "Thank you. I appreciate that." When she pulled away she glanced back at her bag. "Something tells me I don't need pajamas for the evening," she smirked.

Kevin laughed richly. "Nah, I don't think you'll need those. You can always borrow a shirt of mine if you need it."

She nodded. "I've got some clothes for tomorrow, and I just need to grab my toiletries."

"Put on jeans too. You can't ride in shorts. Boots too, if you have them."

Kara nodded and headed for her closet. He watched her pull out a pair of ripped up jeans and combat boots. The night-and-day difference in her appearance from the usual office attire still surprised him. After three years of seeing her so buttoned-up and professional, seeing this side of her was like meeting a new person.

It was fucking hot.

He watched her toss the jeans on the bed and then reach for the button on her jean shorts. She peeled them off her body, revealing smooth, creamy bare skin. He let out a low groan before he was on her. He loved that she was comfortable with him and her body and didn't hide from him.

She let out an "eep" of surprise when he suddenly picked her up and tossed her on the bed.

"Fucking hell, babe." He groaned before he covered her with his body. He kissed her passionately and squeezed the globes of her breasts roughly.

She moaned and arched up against him. He loved the feel of her body against his, soft and supple yet firm. She was easy to toss around and didn't mind when he got rough with her. She loved it.

She worked her hands between them and undid his belt quickly. Her hand was beneath his boxer briefs a moment later, and she gripped him tightly. He groaned and broke the kiss. She knew exactly how to get him off in a few quick moves.

He pulled away before she could get to work, though. "Uh-uh," he smirked. He pushed off her and stood up. He quickly undid his jeans and shoved them down along with his boxers. He grabbed her thighs and yanked her down the mattress until her ass was at the edge. He pulled her thighs far apart and lined up his cock.

He slammed home in one quick thrust before she could even move.

Her eyes rolled back and she moaned loudly.

"God, this pussy is so wet," he breathed as he set a brutal pace. "Derrick treat you right in that bar bathroom?" he asked.

"Yes, so good," she moaned.

He smirked. "You liked Johnny fingering you in the bar for anyone to see?"

She gasped and nodded. "So good."

"Such a dirty little whore," he crooned and fucked her harder.

She cried out at the snap in his hips but didn't object.

"You gonna be our little slut tonight?" he asked.

"Yes," she panted. "Fuck yes."

He smirked. "Going to let us fuck you in every hole? Take this perfect fucking ass?" He laid a hard smack to her ass.

She cried out and arched against him. He quickly regained his grip on her hips and held her in place.

"You going to choke on a cock tonight, baby, while one of us fucks this ass and rails this pussy?" he continued.

Her whole body convulsed around him, shaking and spasming as her orgasm rolled over her. He groaned and rode her through it until she was a whimpering mess beneath him. Only then did he finally let himself go and shoot his load deep in her sopping cunt.

He laughed and leaned down to kiss her. "You liked the sound of that," he said.

Her blush was immediate and covered her face and chest in a deep red. She looked away, and he grabbed her face and pulled her back to look at him.

"It's fucking hot that you like dirty talk so much, baby. Don't be ashamed. And don't be ashamed of what happens tonight. You are not a whore or a slut. You are a fierce woman who enjoys sex. Don't be embarrassed by that."

Her smile was shy and tentative. "How are you so amazing?" she asked, her voice soft. She rubbed a hand over his cheek, her hand grazing over his day-old growth of stubble.

His heart skipped a beat in his chest. His eyes crinkled as he looked down at her. "You're the amazing one, baby," he murmured and pressed a kiss to her lips. "The fact that you haven't gone running for the hills yet or kicked me to the curb is amazing."

She frowned slightly; a wrinkle appeared between her brows. "I wouldn't," she shook her head. "I know this is new still, but these feelings—I've never felt like this about someone before," she said slowly, her eyes darting between his.

He kissed her again. "I feel the same, baby," he said against her lips.

"What about Johnny and Derrick? Won't you get jealous if I'm with one of them and not you?" Her concern made his heart sing.

"No, baby. Sure, we'll have some brotherly competition and rivalry going, to see who can make you come first." He smirked and she blushed. "But it's just in good fun. I meant it when I said we share everything. It just works for us. If one of us can't be there for you, we feel better knowing our brother can be."

She looked pensive so he kissed her again.

Kara was a mess by the time they pulled into the clubhouse yard. She had skipped the panties, per orders from Devil, and then Kevin had rifled through her toy drawer before they left her bedroom to find the stainless steel butt plug with a pink jewel on the end. He had grinned wickedly when he pulled it out, and she'd blushed immediately but nodded. She knew by the end of the night she would sleep with all three of them, so she might as well get relaxed in advance.

Dressed in ripped blue jeans with a seam that sat right on *her seam*, she had laughed thinking of Derrick. The vibrations from the Harley only added to the experience; she wouldn't be surprised if she had soaked through her jeans by the time she slid off the bike. She had been so close to coming on the drive over.

She found herself feeling happy and free for the first time in a long time. She felt more alive and like her old self than she had in years. Sexy and flirty. Her hair was down, and she'd tied a bandanna over the top to try to prevent the wind from knotting it, but she had enjoyed it flying in the breeze.

Kevin pulled up to a long row of bikes outside a long building. He parked near the front of the lineup, in a spot that was left open for him by the looks of it.

When he shut the engine off, she removed her helmet but otherwise didn't move. He glanced over his shoulder at her and smirked. "How you doing, baby?"

She leaned forward and sucked a kiss into his neck, groaning as the plug shifted in her ass.

"Careful now, keep that up and I'll have to bend you over this bike and fuck you in front of everyone." His voice was raspy, like he very much wanted to do just that.

"You wouldn't dare," she declared in his ear.

He let out a low growl. "Keep testing me and find out, woman."

Not wanting to find out, she sighed and let go of him, then slowly got off the bike. She could easily see why it would have been dangerous to ride in shorts. Touching the hot engine and tailpipe could have resulted in nasty burns that would ruined their evening.

She stepped away from the bike to give Kevin room to swing his leg over and stand up. He gave her a sexy grin when he walked toward her and grabbed her hand. "You ready for this?" he asked.

She bit her lower lip and shrugged. "What's there to be ready for? The men in your club to ogle me? Other whores to mark me as competition?" she questioned, suddenly feeling anxious.

"You are not one of those whores," he said fiercely, squeezing her hand. "For one, stop thinking you are because you have three guys chasing after you. Two, those whores would never be allowed to ride bitch on my bike, or Mayhem's or Devil's either. Three—"

She kissed him before he could continue. She was seriously falling in love with this man the more time she spent with him. It had been a whirlwind couple of weeks since they started dating, but she was falling quickly for the tall, dark, and handsome man before her.

The clubhouse was nothing like she thought it'd be. She honestly didn't know what she'd been expecting, but the bar/restaurant she walked into was not it. The room was long and deep. The tables and floor were dark wood, and there were booths along two walls. A very large bar ran the length of the room on the right. Pool tables were stationed near the back half, with dartboards and even a shuffleboard table along the left side. There was a set of black double doors that led to what looked like a conference room, with a massive table in the center of the room. Kevin had called the room church; it was where they discussed club business.

Kara was most surprised by the number of people who hung out in the clubhouse and by just how many people she recognized from work. The foreman of Taylor Construction and Mechanical, Frank Meyers, sat at a table with half his crew, all of whom she recognized.

"This was a bad idea." She groaned, turning to face Kevin just as Johnny walked up.

"Why's that, Princess?" Johnny asked. He cocked a blond eyebrow that made his blue eyes shine.

"Too many people from the office," she said, her eyes wide.

He glanced toward Frank and the others and seemed to realize what had her worried. "Everyone here is loyal to the club. They may not be patched members, but they're only allowed to be here because we trust their loyalty. And they work for me." When she didn't look convinced, Johnny nodded his head toward them. "Come on," he said and grabbed her hand.

Kara hesitated long enough for Johnny to tug her along after him. She sighed, accepting her fate, and plastered a smile on her face.

"Hey Frank, boys." Johnny called out a greeting as he walked up hand in hand with Kara.

She watched as each man looked up to greet them only to then realize who she was. It would have been quite comical if she wasn't so nervous that one of them would blab around the office that she'd been there and who she'd been with.

"Boss, Miss Carmichael," Frank greeted, a pleasant smile on his face.

"Frank," she smiled pleasantly. "Gentlemen." She nodded at the rest of the table of Taylor Construction employees.

"As you can see, Miss Carmichael is here as a guest of mine," Johnny said, his voice deep. "If anyone here makes her feel uncomfortable or anything that happens in here gets back to the office, I will personally cut every single one of your dicks off and shove them down your throats for talking." He spoke so matter-of-factly, as if he were talking about the weather and not threatening to dismember them.

She watched the group of men swallow and look alarmed. "Have a good evening, gentlemen." She grinned, squeezing Johnny's hand.

He smiled brightly and led her away from the table and toward the bar where Derrick was sitting with Kevin. Johnny took the seat beside Kevin and pulled her against him. His hand rested low on her back. "You look amazing," he muttered into her ear before he kissed her neck.

She smiled and leaned against him, letting him wrap his arms around her.

Kevin grinned and handed her a drink. "It's not Macallan," he explained, "but it's not bad."

"Thank you." She smiled gratefully and took a sip. It wasn't bad at all. She nodded and took another sip.

"Stop being a snob," Johnny smirked.

"Excuse me?" she snapped immediately and turned to face him.

He turned to her and rested an elbow on the bar, giving her his full attention. His amusement annoyed her. "Listen here, Johnathan Taylor," she started softly, so no one but the three of them could hear. "You don't know the first damn thing about me. So don't fucking presume to know me."

"Alright, Princess," Johnny drawled, an amused smile on his face. He still wore a baseball cap backward over his blond hair, and his beard was slightly shaggy, like he needed a trim. His baby-blue eyes sparkled with mischief, and it annoyed her to no end. "Enlighten me."

She rolled her eyes and slammed her whisky back. "No," she said and slipped out of his grip. She walked away, sashaying toward a pool table that wasn't being used.

Derrick's riotous laughter followed her.

She started racking for eight-ball. She looked up when Derrick walked over. "You gotta have balls of steel to tell Mayhem no." Derrick laughed as he rounded the table and came up beside her.

She rolled her eyes. "Sounds like he needs to hear it more often."

Derrick slid his hand over her ass and pulled her back against him. She stood up, resting her head back against his shoulder. His hands slid around her hips, gliding over her belly and hips. "You are so fucking beautiful," he breathed into her ear before his mouth latched onto her neck.

She felt like everyone's eyes were on them. Even though they were at one end of the packed room, she felt like she was on display and that everyone knew that she was here for three guys and not just the one she rode in with.

She opened her eyes and found no one paying attention to her, but she did find two very handsome men watching her intently from the bar. She smirked at Johnny and tilted her head up and to her right.

Derrick released her neck and captured her lips immediately. When they broke apart, breathless, a moment later, Derrick said. "You're playing with fire, baby girl." Then he smacked her ass and stepped away from her.

She shrugged. "Pool?"

He grinned wickedly and nodded.

# Chapter Eleven

J OHNNY WATCHED HER FROM across the clubhouse. She was actually pretty fucking good at pool—gave Derrick a run for his money and even won a game or two. She seemed to be having a good time toying with him from across the room.

At one point Devil pulled out what appeared to be her panties and waved them around in the air, much to both her and Johnny's annoyance.

Kara glared across the barroom when a courtesan flounced her way over to Johnny and tried to come on to him. He had allowed it for a few minutes, to rile up Kara, but he wasn't about to let it get out of hand.

"You just have to goad her." Kevin shook his head and took a sip of his beer.

Johnny smirked and shrugged. "She gets so fired up. It's fucking hot."

"There's firing her up and there's mocking her. She's right you know; you really don't know the first thing about her."

Johnny looked over at his friend and met his stare. He knew there was more to her than met the eye—the two sleeves of tattoos made that obvious—but what was Kevin alluding to? "Alright, man," he agreed. "I'll lay off."

Kevin nodded and then walked over to where Kara was sucking on a straw seductively while eye fucking him and Johnny. Devil was behind her again, hands on her hips.

Johnny watched as Kevin walked over to them. Rockstar took the glass out of Kara's hands and wrapped a hand around her jaw. He leaned over her much smaller frame and kissed her deeply. Even from across the bar, Johnny could see the liquid drip down her chin as Kevin sucked her drink from her mouth.

*So fucking hot.*

Devil was attached to her back, mouth on her neck again. His hands inched up her tank top, putting the bare skin of her abdomen on display. As a tattoo peaked out over her jeans, Johnny knew he was a goner. *How the hell did this prim and proper CEO have so many damn tattoos?*

Kevin's hands slid down her body and cupped the underside of her breasts. His thumbs circled her nipples, pinching them between his thumb and forefinger.

Johnny couldn't hear her moan across the room, not over all the other women moaning and writhing on the laps of his brothers, but he watched Kara arch her back, pushing her tits into Kevin's hands. Devil undid the top button of her jeans and slid his hand inside.

Johnny couldn't believe how much she'd let them get away with already today. He'd fingered her in the restaurant at dinner after Devil had fucked her in the bathroom. This was just a whole other level of *unreal* that Johnny didn't believe the Ice Queen had up her sleeves.

Maybe he needed to stop imagining what he thought she was like and actually go find out what she was *really* like.

Johnny glanced around the room and noticed a few of his guys from the Taylor Construction crew hanging around still. They were eyeing the show Kara was unknowingly putting on with blatant stares.

It appeared Johnny wasn't the only one surprised that Miss Prim and Proper could be so bold. He didn't like them leering at his woman, though, so he got up and headed their way. "About time you boys headed out, isn't it?" Johnny asked, stopping at their table.

Chris and Jack jumped, clearly startled to find him in front of them. Johnny crossed his arms and waited. "Right. Yep. Night, boss," one of them muttered. They scrambled from the table and tossed money down.

Johnny didn't wait to make sure they were gone; he headed for where Rockstar and Devil had Kara sandwiched between them. Devil's hand was fully in her jeans now. His finger was probably buried in her cunt, working her over.

Rockstar was squeezing her breasts and pinching her nipples.

Kara's head was tossed back on Devil's shoulder. Her blue eyes were closed tight. Her mouth parted as she panted. Johnny didn't hear Rockstar until he got up to them, but he was whispering a litany of dirty things to her. "Fucking beautiful slut. Our little whore. Can't get enough of it, can you baby? Don't care that anyone could be watching you, Devil fucking you with his fingers."

Kara panted and gasped when Johnny gripped her jaw and turned her toward him. Her eyes snapped open and flew to his.

Kevin kept talking. "Tell me little slut, has Devil found the plug in your ass yet?"

Devil looked to Kevin with a wild grin and then must have slid his fingers further back because he groaned deeply. "Fucking hell, you dirty girl." He growled into her ear and ground his cock against her ass.

She whimpered, but Johnny held her jaw, preventing her from moving. "You like that, Princess?" Johnny asked. "You want the three of us to fuck this sexy body in all of your holes? Make you scream?"

Her mouth dropped open and he squeezed her jaw tighter. A moan escaped her as he shoved two fingers from his other hand between her open lips. She immediately sucked and closed her eyes.

"Uh-uh, Princess," he tsked. He pressed down on her tongue with his fingers and forced her mouth open wider. "You look at me when you suck me."

Her eyes popped open. Her pupils were blown wide. Something he'd noted it at dinner. His little slut was submissive. He would need to be careful with her. They would need to speak about limits immediately.

He let up on her tongue and she immediately closed her mouth around his fingers again and started sucking hard, her eyes on his.

"Come for me, baby girl," Devil commanded in her ear.

Kevin pinched her nipples tightly.

She groaned and shuddered immediately. Her body arched and her eyes started to droop before she quickly snapped them open and kept them on Johnny's. Pride filled him. She had remembered his orders in the middle of an orgasm. She would be worth training if that was something they wanted to explore further.

"Good girl," Johnny praised. "Such a good girl for us. Coming on command, remembering to look at me while you suck me. Good girl."

"Why don't we take this party somewhere more comfortable?" Kevin suggested.

Johnny nodded. "My room is the biggest." He pulled his fingers out of Kara's mouth and quickly kissed her. Her hand came up and slid through the scruff on his jaw. She held him to her for a moment as Devil buttoned up her pants.

Johnny broke the kiss before it could turn heated. They needed to move. He needed to be inside her *now*. He pried her out of Derrick's and Kevin's arms and picked her up. She immediately wrapped her legs around his waist, and he groaned as her crotch hit his. "Fucking *Christ*," he cursed and took off for the back of the barroom.

He headed down the long hallway just past church that led to the dorms. There was a staircase halfway down, and Johnny climbed the stairs as quickly as he could with Kara in his arms. She latched onto his neck and ground her hips against his.

He laid a heavy smack to her ass when he reached the midpoint landing and turned to continue up to the second floor. "Stop that," he growled.

Her laugh was low and melodic in his ear.

He was a goner. Such a fucking goner.

He went left at the top of the stairs and headed down the long hall to the last door. His suite at the clubhouse as vice president was on the opposite end of the hall from his father's and about as far away from the main barroom of the clubhouse as you could get. It ensured quiet, and tonight he would want the privacy.

He pushed open the door. His suite was really just an extra-large bedroom that was split into two areas that he had separated by dressers. One side he had set up as a living room, with a couple couches and a La-Z-Boy recliner that were centered around a large TV. On the other side he had a king-size bed and a couple nightstands. The bed faced another large TV. He had his own bathroom, and on the wall behind his living room he set up a countertop with cabinets. He had a microwave and minifridge and even a coffee pot for days he didn't want to head down to the main room too early.

It wasn't much, but it was more than most of the dorm rooms offered in the clubhouse.

Johnny carried Kara straight to the bed. Thankfully the courtesans had changed the sheets recently. He set Kara down on the edge of the bed and stepped back. They would discuss limits first, even if it killed him.

She frowned when he stepped back and Kevin and Derrick stepped in next to him. They seemed to be on the same page here. "Why are you guys just standing there?" she asked, looking up at the three of them.

"Before we do anything further, we need to discuss limits," Johnny said.

She frowned, eyes widening.

"Today might have gone a little further than any of us intended, and we need to make sure we haven't crossed any lines," Johnny continued.

Her lips parted, forming a perfect O before she smiled and slowly got to her feet. "Because fingering me in front of your entire clubhouse, your brothers, might have crossed a line?" she asked, stepping toward them.

"Shit," Derrick groaned.

"Yeah, something like that." Johnny nodded.

Kevin shifted. "Kara, we don't want to cross lines or make you uncomfortable, so you need to tell us. Hard limits?" he asked.

"No face slapping," she said immediately.

Johnny nodded. "What else?"

She hesitated and glanced away.

Johnny moved into her space. He put a finger under her chin and gently lifted her face to meet his gaze. "What else, Princess?"

"I don't—I don't like being degraded outside of us playing," she admitted. "I was fine with dinner and downstairs." She turned to Kevin and nodded. "I know you don't really think that. And it's hot when we're playing, but I don't want to hear it outside of that."

"Perfectly understandable," Johnny nodded. "What else?"

She closed her eyes before she continued. "I have trust issues." She sighed. "I've been cheated on before and I don't—" she shook her head and slowly opened her eyes. "I know it's not fair that I get all three of you, and you only get—"

"Don't you dare finish that sentence." Derrick growled, his green eyes narrowed.

Kara blushed when she met his intense stare, but she glanced back at Johnny. "I just, I need to know that there won't be other women."

He felt it like a blow to the gut. The pain in her eyes, the uncertainty there. He had done that. By letting the courtesan linger and flirt, he had put that doubt and uncertainty in her heart. "Absolutely not," he said vehemently. "You won't have to worry about that. I'm sorry if I made you feel doubt tonight. I'm sorry for my part in that. It won't happen again."

She searched his eyes, looking for the truth, before she nodded slowly. "Thank you." She moved toward him and pressed a soft kiss to his lips.

He cradled her face between his hands and kissed her again when she tried to pull away. "What else, baby?" he asked.

She smiled softly. "Public displays. Dinner and outside the bar on the street were close to too much," she admitted. "Out there in the clubhouse, that was hot, but I don't think I could do any more than that. And my job—if anything got out, it could be extremely damaging to my career."

Johnny once again felt like an ass. He had pushed some of that earlier and hadn't even thought about her career. She wasn't just a lawyer but also the managing partner of the most prestigious law firm in the city. He nodded. "Noted. We'll be careful from now on."

Her smile was beautiful and heartwarming. "Other than that, I don't really have any other limits. I like to be choked and I like it rough." She giggled. "Don't be afraid of breaking me. But I also like to be checked in on once in a while."

Johnny smiled easily. She was so brave and strong. She knew what she wanted and wasn't afraid to tell him what she needed. "We can do that, Princess." He nodded.

"Safe words?" Derrick asked.

Her eyes widened slightly and a blush bloomed across her cheeks before she quickly glanced at Kevin, who nodded and smirked, and then looked back to Derrick. "Uh, red to stop, yellow to slow down, green for good."

"Perfect." Derrick smiled.

*Perfect, indeed,* Johnny thought. She was utterly perfect in every sense of the word. She would be his undoing and downfall. He knew it.

# Chapter Twelve

Kara couldn't believe the turn the night had taken. The discussion of limits was not foreign to her. She'd experimented with boyfriends in the past, and she and Kevin had already had a brief discussion, but this was something *more*.

Johnny had been so serious. Still seemed so serious.

She knew she had to do something to change the atmosphere. She looked up at Johnny and slowly dropped to her knees. Hearing his groan as she landed gracefully on the floor, legs beneath her, was worth it. She pushed her shoulders back, rested her hands on her knees, palms up, lowered her gaze to the floor, and waited.

"Fuck me," Johnny groaned softly. His voice was like gravel.

She couldn't keep the smirk off her lips if she tried. She absolutely loved that she was making him come undone.

"There's my good slut," Kevin crooned and started circling her. "Been so good all day," he continued, his voice like velvet.

Shivers raced down her spine—she could listen to his voice all day. Rich and smooth. Silky. He knew just how wet she got from listening to him talk dirty. One day she would record his voice just so she could listen to it on days when she couldn't see him.

"Please, Sir," she murmured.

"Please, what?" Kevin fisted a hand into her hair and pulled her head back. He stood behind her, so she had to crane her head up far to see him.

"Please touch me," she breathed. "Fuck me. Use me."

"Such a greedy little slut," Kevin chuckled darkly. "I don't know. You've been awfully insatiable today. What do we get in return?"

"Me." She smiled up at him. "You get me any way you want me."

He grinned down at her wickedly. Butterflies danced in her stomach. Kevin's dark eyes turned black, and he yanked her hair tighter. "That's right little whore. We get you. We own you now. There's no turning back. You belong to me and my brothers."

He pulled her roughly to her feet by her hair. "Yesss," she hissed.

"Good girl." Johnny pressed against her front and grabbed her jaw.

She whimpered into his kiss as he angled her head to meet his lips, her hair still fisted in Kevin's hand.

Another set of hands was on her jeans, quickly undoing the button of her pants. She was swiftly shed of all her clothing before she was picked up by Johnny and laid in the center of the bed reverently. She was already panting as a hand kneaded her breast and tongues flicked over her nipples.

"Please," she breathed as someone kissed their way down to her core.

She tried to thread her fingers through their hair and guide their head where she needed it, but her hands were quickly snatched up. "Uh-uh," Derrick said and lifted her hands above her head.

She moaned as a mouth latched onto her clit. She heard the snick of a belt being slid out of jeans before it was looped around her wrists and tightened. Once it was secured to the headboard, she tested the strength. There was some give to it. She could probably get out if she really wanted to.

"Don't move them," Kevin commanded, his voice inches from her ears.

"Yes, Sir," she murmured.

"Good girl," Kevin praised.

She kept her eyes closed, afraid that if she opened them, it wouldn't be real. She'd never done anything like this before—slept with three men at once. Her heart raced as butterflies danced in her stomach. Every touch was like fire to her nerves.

Fingers entered her core. Two hot mouths latched on to her nipples. She gasped and arched her back. Hands gripped her hips, just shy of painful, and held her down. Someone—Derrick—kissed her deeply as the two fingers in her cunt curled upward and rubbed circles into her G-spot.

A hand wrapped around her throat, cutting off her air supply, and she gasped into the kiss, tears pouring down her face as her body shuddered against the hands holding her in place. The orgasm that tore out of her had her seeing stars.

The hand around her throat released her, and she gasped into Derrick's kiss. "Good girl," he murmured as he broke the kiss.

Her eyes slid open slowly. The lights in the room had been dimmed. Her boys were already naked, Kevin to her right, Derrick to her left, and Johnny between her thighs. "More, please," she panted, seeing them in all their glory.

Johnny gave a sinful grin. "Does the little slut need more?"

"Please," she begged, rolling her hips.

She watched his baby-blue eyes darken with desire. His sinful smile turned into a feral smirk. "Let her hands go," Johnny ordered.

Kevin reached for the belt and quickly released her wrists, rubbing them to return the circulation and make sure she wasn't hurt.

Johnny knelt between her legs, and she was able to see his impressive length for the first time. He was *huge.* Her mouth dropped open as Johnny grabbed her wrists from Kevin and pulled her up so she was sitting with her face inches from his bobbing cock.

He took advantage of her open mouth and slid his cock between her lips. He hissed when she wrapped her lips around his head. Encouraged by his response, she wrapped a hand around his base, as much as she could, and gripped his balls with her other hand. "Fuck," he groaned when she sucked him in deep. "That's it, Princess." He panted. "Put that mouth to work."

Johnny's hand fisted in her hair and yanked her down his cock. He held her down as she started sputtering around his dick. "Breathe," he ordered.

She took a deep breath through her nose and let it out slowly. She continued to breathe deeply, and Johnny remained still to allow her to get used to him in the back of her throat.

"Good girl," he praised when she finally relaxed her throat.

Kevin and Derrick went back to work on her body. Fingers entered her cunt again, while others twisted and pinched her nipples. She moaned deeply around Johnny's cock when someone's thumb circled her clit.

"Fuck yes, Princess," Johnny growled and started moving her head on his cock.

She no longer had control. He moved her head as he wanted and thrust into her mouth at the same time, truly fucking her throat. He pulled her with him as he backed up a foot, so she had to scramble to get on her hands and knees. The position allowed him to sink deeper into her throat.

"Goddamn, that's hot," Derrick groaned.

A hand came down on her ass. The loud smack startled her and forced her further onto Johnny's cock. They both groaned as she slid the last inch down his dick and her nose pressed against his abdomen. The plug in her ass was jostled deeper. She had almost forgotten it was there until she was spanked.

"That's it, Princess." Johnny grunted. "Stay right there for just a little longer."

Breathing was hard, but she forced her throat to relax around his cock. It was stretching her in ways she never imagined before. His skin smelled fresh and clean, with a hint of leather and sandalwood.

Fingers slid through her folds. "Such a messy whore, she is," Derrick rasped. "And this plug is so pretty," he murmured, rubbing a thumb over the pink jewel. "Such a good girl. You got this ass ready for me."

Kara groaned when he slowly pulled out the butt plug before two fingers quickly replaced them and slid into her back passage. There was a pop of a cap opening before cool liquid was drizzled onto and into her puckered hole. She gasped and arched, sliding against Johnny's cock.

"Fuck, Princess." He groaned. His hands gripped either side of her face and held her in place. She was trapped, whether she wanted to move or not. He held her pressed against his torso so tightly that breathing was difficult. "Relax," he ordered.

She had no choice but to listen or suffocate.

"Kara, you tap his leg if it becomes too much, alright?" Kevin said.

She tried to nod but ended up giving him a thumbs-up instead.

"Good girl," Derrick murmured.

Her pussy clenched down on nothing while the fingers in her ass scissored her open.

"How you doing, Kara?" Johnny asked softly. He pulled back slightly, permitting her to breathe easier.

She opened her eyes to find his blue eyes shining down at her with a look of reverence. She slid her hand up his thigh and rubbed over his rock-hard abs.

He lifted her hand to his mouth and pressed a kiss against her knuckles. She tried to smile around his cock but couldn't. So when he released her hand, she slid it down his body and between them and cupped his balls. "Oh fuck." He groaned as his own eyes rolled back in his head.

"Hold up," Kevin muttered, and she was shifted again. He laid down next to her, and the boys carefully moved her to straddle him.

She groaned as his cock slid between her folds and slipped inside. He didn't give her any time to adjust, just gripped her hips roughly and slammed in to the hilt.

The force jolted her forward on Johnny's length, and she groaned when he slipped further down her throat again. Johnny grunted and she shuddered. Her orgasm was so close. Everything about the scene they were playing out had her on edge.

Derrick was still scissoring his fingers in her ass, and there was another dollop of lube poured over and inside her open hole before the thick head of his cock replaced his fingers and slid past the ring of muscles.

She whined and came immediately, every nerve ending firing off at once. She shuddered and groaned and swallowed thickly around Johnny's cock. "Fuck, I'm not gonna last much longer," he groaned.

Kara was in a daze as Derrick bottomed out in her ass while her orgasm squeezed and shook and rocked her body.

The three of them gave her a moment to catch her breath and come down from her high before they kicked it into gear and found a rhythm. Thrusting and pulling, the three of them used her body so thoroughly she couldn't think.

Her mind felt empty. Her body was light and tingly. She felt like she was floating. Fingers clamped down on her nipples and pressed her clit. When another orgasm was forced out of her, all three of her boys groaned in unison. Johnny pulled his cock out of her throat to come in her mouth and coat her lips. Cum dribbled out of her mouth as she tried to swallow the thick spurts of it.

She was still shaking and shuddering when Johnny pulled out of her mouth, scooped up the cum from her chin, and slid his fingers in her mouth. He praised her as she sucked his fingers.

She collapsed onto Kevin's chest a moment later when her legs finally gave out. She was boneless and sleepy and utterly spent.

"Good girl, Kara," Kevin murmured into her hair before he pressed a kiss to her forehead.

"So good for us, babe," Derrick murmured and pressed a kiss to her shoulder before he slowly eased out of her.

She groaned faintly. "Water," she muttered.

A moment later, Kevin was sitting up with her cradled against him, cock still inside her, while Johnny tilted a glass against her lips. She sipped the cool water as her mind slowly came back online. Her body ached, her throat was raw, but she'd never before been so *satiated*. She felt amazing.

"How you doing, Princess?" Johnny asked softly as he pulled the glass away from her.

She gave him a sleepy smile and reached up for him. He met her halfway and pressed his lips gently to hers. "Good," she moaned, against his mouth.

He grinned and pulled away. "Let's get you cleaned up."

"Sleep," she groaned instead.

Kevin chuckled and shifted beneath her. Strong hands wrapped around her waist as both Kevin and Johnny lifted her from Kevin's lap.

She groaned but sighed when she was laid down on the bed, head propped on a pillow. A moment later, a warm cloth wiped through her folds, cleaning her. Derrick, her mind registered. "Sleep," someone said.

She didn't need to be told twice. She was out a moment later, glorious darkness claiming her.

She woke sometime later to the feeling of being fucked. She was straddling someone in the dark, and another was already in her ass. She let out a low moan and arched her back. Hands were on her breasts and hips, holding her in place.

"That's it, baby," Kevin murmured in her ear from behind her.

"Your fucking cunt is fantastic, Princess." Johnny groaned from beneath her.

She smirked and swiveled her hips. They both moaned deeply.

"Open up, baby girl," Derrick said before his cock pressed against her lips. She had a quick thought of him being in her ass earlier and jerked away. "Relax, I showered." He chuckled before he pressed his cock between her lips.

She groaned as she tasted clean skin. He smelled vaguely of Johnny's sandalwood and leather. Probably used his bodywash, she thought as she sucked him down. Her jaw was still sore, but she sucked him down deep.

A thumb pressed against her clit, and she moaned around Derrick's cock.

"So fucking perfect, Princess," Johnny panted.

She swiveled her hips again and grabbed Derrick's balls as she forced his cock down her throat. Kevin's mouth latched onto her neck, and he bit down as he twisted her nipples; Johnny rubbed her clit, and together they worked her over the edge of her umpteenth orgasm of the night.

The three of them came groaning a moment later as their orgasms tore through them. Derrick came down her throat; she barely tasted him when he pulled out of her. She collapsed onto Johnny's chest and snuggled in against him.

Kevin pulled out slowly, and Derrick was already there with a warm washcloth. "Are you gonna pull out?" Derrick asked.

Johnny grunted but slowly lifted Kara's hips off his and slid out of her.

Derrick wiped the warm washcloth over Kara's cunt before he handed it to Johnny to clean himself off.

Kara didn't pay much attention after that. She drifted off to sleep tucked under Johnny's arm.

The next morning, Kara woke slowly. Her body felt languid and sore. She was relaxed and comfortable. Her head still rested on someone's shoulder. Arms were wrapped around her. There was a delicious ache in most of her muscles and hips. She felt like she had run a marathon last night.

She rolled onto her back and stretched as much as she could between two hard male bodies. She yawned as a hand slid over her belly. She arched her back and smiled as it cracked in several places.

"Morning, beautiful Princess." Johnny's voice was raspy in her ear as he rolled onto his side and curled around her.

She smiled and opened her eyes slowly to see his face inches from hers. She turned her head and pressed a kiss to his lips.

"How are you feeling?" Kevin asked from her left. He curled around her other side, propped his head up on his hand, and smiled down at her.

"Good. Sore, like I had the workout of my life, but good." She smiled at him.

His hair was sleep tousled, but his brown eyes were bright and crinkled in the corners when he smiled at her. He leaned down and kissed her softly. "Let's go out for breakfast," he suggested.

"Sounds great to me." Derrick groaned from the other side of Kevin.

Kara giggled and nodded. "I'm good with that."

It was slow moving after that. The boys helped Kara into the shower and then gave her some space to shower in peace...until Johnny walked in while she was washing her hair.

She jumped when hands slid down her slick body.

"Easy, Princess," Johnny's deep voice murmured.

"I thought you were giving me privacy?" she smirked.

"Well, Kevin and Derrick headed back to their dorm rooms to shower...and since you're in mine..." he chuckled. "Conserving water and all that."

Kara giggled but allowed him to pull her into his arms and kissed him back when his mouth claimed hers. It didn't take long for the kiss to turn passionate. Kara groaned as Johnny tilted her head back and ran his fingers through her hair to help rinse it of shampoo while never breaking the kiss.

She broke the kiss, panting, and finished rinsing. She refused to be distracted while doing her hair-care routine, even if she didn't have her shampoo and conditioner. Johnny at least didn't use an all-in-one, one-size-cleans-all-man bodywash. So she washed her hair with his fancy shampoo and was grateful it would do until she could wash it with her good products.

Johnny's hands continued to roam her body. His mouth latched onto her neck, making her groan. She hadn't looked in the mirror to see how many hickeys and bruises her men had sucked into her skin the last twenty-four hours.

"Goddamn, Princess." Johnny groaned into her skin. "How are you so utterly perfect?"

She smiled and shook her head. "Funny, that's not what you're usually saying."

She opened her eyes to see his blue eyes raw and exposed. She gasped when she saw the emotion on his face. He meant what he said. He cupped her face and rubbed her cheek with his thumb.

Her heart sped up. He was so intense all the time, and he towered over her, making her feel tiny compared to him. His shoulders were broad and muscular—he was easily twice as wide as her. His thick arms were covered in multicolored tattoos: skulls and skeletons and the Ravager Knights logo with its menacing skeleton in armor holding a scythe above their motto: "Death's Henchmen *to deliver your soul to Death himself.*"

Some of their other mottos were intertwined in his skin along with the words "United Psychos," that only he, Kevin, and Derrick were a part of.

She ran her hands over his arms and chest, marveling at the chiseled muscles. "Come here, pretty lady." Johnny's voice was gruff.

She looked back up at him, taking in his buzzed blond hair and slightly grown out beard. It was due for a trim, but she loved that little bit of extra ruggedness the beard gave him. It added to his dangerous appeal.

He pulled her toward him and kissed her soundly. She melted against him. She let the kiss turn filthy as he sucked her tongue into his mouth. She slid her hands around his shoulders and let out a little "eep" when he picked her up and her back hit the cold tile wall. She wrapped her legs around his waist and held on tight.

He gripped under her thighs and shifted her; she felt his hard cock bob against her abdomen before he lined himself up. She reached between them, gripped his length, and guided him into her core.

She threw her head back against the wall and groaned as he sunk in deep in one slow thrust. "Johnny." She moaned, digging her fingers into his shoulders.

"Fuck, Princess." He gasped. "Your pussy is amazing."

She smirked. "I bet you say that to all the whores you fuck," she joked.

He stopped moving and grew serious. She watched the change come over his face. "Kara," he said, his voice low. "You know you aren't one of those whores to me, right? That *this*," he motioned between the two of them, "means something?"

She opened her mouth to say something but was lost for words. What did you say to something like that? It wasn't a declaration of love. But it was definitely feelings. She cleared her throat. "I think I know that?" she started. "I know you said last night that I would be enough for you and that you were mine... I just... I'm sorry," she sighed.

He was patient though and didn't speak. He let her gather her thoughts.

"This is just so new still—the idea that three men want *me*. It's hard to wrap my head around that any of this is real; I'm no one special," she admitted softly.

Johnny's thumb rubbed over her cheekbone as he watched her silently. His blue eyes were stony. "I'm going to kill whoever it was that made you question that *anyone* wouldn't want you." He growled. "Then I'm going to serve them to you on a silver platter so you never forget *your worth*."

Kara cut him off with a kiss before he could continue. He growled and cradled her head and deepened the kiss. It wasn't long before he was thrusting into her again. He didn't rush things, though. For as fiery as his kiss had been, he slowed things down to match his thrusts. Slow and sensual.

It was probably as close to lovemaking as a man like Johnny could get.

She clung to him and let him lead. When she broke the kiss, chanting his name softly, he picked up the pace. "Johnny!" She cried out when she came, her walls fluttering around his cock, milking him for all he was worth.

He groaned not long after her, snapping his hips against hers and grunting as he spilled inside her.

They were both breathless as he slowly lowered her to the shower floor. He rested his head on his forearm over her head and gasped for breath. She leaned back against the shower wall, not trusting her legs to support her weight, and panted.

"Johnny," she murmured, sliding a hand down his chest.

"Yeah baby?"

"Thank you." She didn't elaborate, felt she didn't need to. They had been so in tune while alone in the shower.

He leaned down and pressed a kiss to her forehead. "This might be new still," his voice was gravelly, "but I promise you, I will show you just how special you are to me." He cupped the back of her neck and stared deep into her eyes as he spoke the words like a vow to her.

She bit her lower lip and nodded, watching him.

He brushed his thumb over her lower lip, pulling it from her teeth, before he pressed a kiss to her lips.

# Chapter Thirteen

T HE TWO WEEKS FOLLOWING her night spent at the club-house were busy. The boys had started to make themselves at home at Kara's house. Usually, one or all three of them spent the night any given night of the week.

Kara had to lay down some rules for weeknights, though. She had work to do, and it wouldn't be seemly if she was covered in hickeys and a walking zombie in the office. There were still too many spies of her father's loitering around.

The boys had agreed, and while they were still able to have their fun, they mostly left her alone once she passed out for the evening.

She had had to upgrade her bed too. The little queen mattress was not enough for the four of them to fit in comfortably. They had made a trip to the bedding store downtown and picked out one of those fancy Alaskan king mattresses. The boys had bitched about the price and said a king would do, but she just smiled and handed over her black card to the sales rep.

When the bed was delivered later that same day and they had thoroughly christened it, her men relented and said it was worth the money.

While the four of them were learning each other's routines and boundaries in the evenings and weekends, during the day, Kara had begun digging into Case Holdings, Mac Taylor's shell company, which he allegedly was using to embezzle money from Granger Ltd., one of the firm's clients.

As CEO and managing partner for Carmichael and Associates, Kara felt it was her responsibility to know what was happening when one of their biggest clients was pressing charges for racketeering, embezzlement, money laundering, and fraud.

It didn't surprise her to find out that Ken Laraway was their attorney. He probably didn't even tell them that he'd been fired from Carmichael and Associates. Or maybe he did and this was another bylaw broken by him. Poaching clients.

She found that the more she dug into Case Holdings and the Granger case, the more dead ends and brick walls she slammed against. She even went so far as to hire Stonewall Financials, the number one forensic accounting firm in the country, to dig into the Carmichael accounts. She wanted a full audit done and needed it done discreetly.

Thankfully her very good friend Stephanie Stonewall happened to own the company and would keep things as discreet as she possibly could, but it would take her some time.

Kara didn't like it, but she didn't have a choice. While she waited for Stephanie to do her thing, Kara reached out to Freddy Danvers, with Johnny's blessing of course, and set up a meeting.

Freddy Danvers was legendary in the courtroom. He was roughly her father's age, early sixties. He was fit and filled out his tailored Tom Ford suit to perfection. He was an attractive man, with gray eyes that seemed to pierce right through you. His black hair was just starting to gray at the temples, and he was clean-shaven with a hint of a five-o'clock shadow on his jaw.

"Miss Carmichael." He greeted her with a sharklike smile when she walked in ten minutes early. He stood and shook her hand and was completely cordial. He sat across the table from her at Supérieur, a posh French restaurant downtown, looking for all the world like a king in his castle. She was immediately put off by his exuberant *show*. But she sat down across from him and played nice.

She had called for this meeting after all.

They kept talk light until they ordered their meals, then he finally turned the conversation toward the matter at hand. "So why do you want to meet my client?" He cut right to the chase.

"I thought I could help you," she started, not quite liking his gruff persona. She was used to his type, though. She met them and *crushed* them daily in the courtroom. It had rubbed her the wrong way when she had called him to arrange a meeting with Mac Taylor, offering her assistance, and he had invited her to this *luncheon* instead.

Interrogation was more like it.

"I didn't realize you had been practicing criminal law as of late, Miss Carmichael," Freddy Danvers drawled.

She narrowed her eyes at the man. "Not particularly, but all laws can become criminal with the right incentive."

He tipped his head at her in acquiescence. "And what brings the great Kara Carmichael, CEO and managing partner of Carmichael and Associates, down to mingle with the lowly criminal underbelly?"

"I'll be real with you, Freddy. I'm dating Johnny Taylor." She left it at that, not elaborating further.

Danvers narrowed his gaze on her, letting it roam over her face, as if reassessing her again. "I did not see that one coming," He nodded toward her. She could see his persona shift as the airs were dropped. "Alright then. What do you know?"

"Not enough," she answered immediately, ignoring that he'd finally come around. Men like him were a dime a dozen. "I know that Mac is being accused of crimes he didn't commit. I know that Case Holdings *shouldn't* be an active company. But it sounds like Mac didn't give you much to go on," Kara said.

"No. He kept stating that he didn't do it. That he registered the company forty years ago and never did anything with it." Freddy shook his head and scratched his eyebrow. "We both know clients will say anything to get out of taking blame."

Kara nodded slowly. "I have some information I'd like to run by Mac. I would like to speak to him."

Freddy narrowed his gaze on her again. She was beyond sick of men underestimating her. "And I don't suppose you'll tell me whatever it is?"

She smiled sweetly. "No."

Freddy let out a booming laugh and tipped his head toward her. "Alright, Miss Carmichael," he drawled. "I'll set up the meeting. If what you have is solid, we'll discuss your involvement in my case."

Kara rolled her eyes but held out her hand.

Freddy shook it almost reluctantly.

She smiled sweetly. "I look forward to your call," she said and stood up.

Freddy smirked and nodded as their waitress set their food on the table before them.

"Thanks for lunch," she added with a smile, then slung her Louis Vuitton purse over her shoulder and walked away.

She had things to do, and entertaining a man like Freddy Danvers was not one of them.

A week later, Kara found herself pulling into the parking lot of the county jail for a meeting with Mac Taylor. Mourningside County Correctional was your standard county jail. Lots of concrete and chain-link fencing surrounded a concrete building with tiny windows. Danvers was waiting for her out front; she had turned down his offer to ride together. She didn't need to be trapped in a car with the man if she didn't absolutely need to be.

"Good morning, Miss Carmichael." Danvers smiled cordially when she approached him at the gate. He was dressed in another of his Tom Ford suits, this one gray with a navy-blue shirt, which brought out his gray eyes.

"Good morning, Freddy." She grinned and walked past him toward the guard at the gate. She had dressed in a pants suit and opted for flats instead of her usual heels. The guards tried to make things as safe as possible for attorneys visiting clients, but it never hurt to wear sensible shoes and clothing when going into a dangerous environment.

After showing their IDs and walking through the metal detectors, she and Danvers were escorted to an interview room that was little more than a ten-by-ten holding cell with a steel table and three chairs in the center of the room.

Kara set down her briefcase on the table, pulled out a writing pad and a pen before she sat down, and set her briefcase on the floor. She pulled out a recording device from her pocket and set it on the table.

She raised an eyebrow when Danvers only pulled out a recording device from his pocket and set it on the table.

"You have your process, I have mine," he said when he noticed her stare.

She shrugged but didn't comment as the door was opened. In walked a man with the same blue eyes and blond beard as Johnny, but that's where the similarities ended. Mac wasn't as tall as Johnny, nor was he as fit as his son. He was beefy, with a soft belly and a barrel chest. He might have been fit at one time, but he'd let himself go with age.

From the file Danvers had sent her during the week, she knew he was sixty-five and had been diagnosed with COPD from years of smoking.

Mac gave her a shrewd look as his gaze raked over her face and trailed down her body.

She leveled a look at him that he finally noticed when his gaze reached hers again. He smirked, clearly unbothered by her annoyance. "Mr. Taylor, I'm Kara Carmichael," she introduced herself, getting straight to the point.

His smirk dropped from his face, and he glared immediately.

She smirked in return and continued before he could speak up. "I'm currently dating your son, and I'm here on his behalf."

"I find that hard to believe," Mac growled.

Kara smirked and pulled out her phone. She quickly FaceTimed Johnny, turning the phone so Mac would be on camera and not her. Thankfully Johnny answered immediately, as he had agreed to her plan earlier. "Dad," Johnny greeted.

"Johnny," Mac's voice was gruff, and he leaned forward to be closer to the screen.

"Hey, Dad. I know what you're thinking about a Carmichael being on our side, but I trust Kara. She's one of the good ones, you know?"

Mac glanced at Kara, who waited patiently, courtroom-stone-wall face in place. "Alright," Mac nodded slowly.

"And Dad," Johnny added. "She's special to me, so play nice."

Mac's eyes narrowed on the phone; Kara watched as his demeanor slowly grew suspicious. "Alright," he said again.

*A man of few words.*

"Call me when you can. We've got shit to discuss," Johnny added.

Mac rolled his eyes. "They record everything; you know that. But if you swing by my house, you'll find a notebook on my desk with everything you need."

"Alright," Kara heard Johnny shuffling, heard the telltale scritch of him scratching his beard. "You OK?"

"Fine," Mac grunted.

Kara rolled her eyes and didn't care if Mac saw her. She was over the macho-man bullshit. She turned the phone around and smiled at Johnny. He gave her an exasperated look and shook his head.

She smiled at her man and nodded. "You'll be by for dinner?" she asked, not caring if Mac or Danvers was watching.

"Yeah, Princess. I'll see you tonight."

Kara smiled and said goodbye, ending the call. She put her phone in her pocket and turned her gaze to Mac. "Shall we begin?" she asked pleasantly.

"You're really dating my son?" Mac asked.

"For several weeks now," Kara answered.

Mac opened his mouth to say something more but glanced at Danvers. Instead, he raised an eyebrow at Kara and asked, "How are Rockstar and Devil?"

Kara smiled easily. "They are great. One big happy family."

Mac laughed gruffly and shook his head. "And you're just here out of the goodness of your heart?" he asked.

"I'm here because Johnny asked me to be. But I'm also here because I have questions for you." She held up her recording device and made a show of turning it on in front of him. "For instance, what is your relationship with my father?"

Mac barked another laugh. "Right for the gut, huh?"

She smiled plainly and waited.

"What is *your* relationship with your father?" Mac shot back.

"I met my father for the first time ten years ago," Kara answered honestly. "He called me six months after my mother died. Couldn't even come to her funeral. Our relationship is...*rocky* at best."

Mac's eyes narrowed as she spoke. The smile turned into a sneer. "But yet you still became CEO and managing partner of his prestigious law firm. Oh, woe is me," he drawled.

She smiled and shrugged. "Sure did," she deadpanned.

"Alright, *Princess*," he said almost condescendingly, "I'll play. Your father and I used to be good friends until he fucked my fiancée and got her pregnant. She left me for him. Had a little boy, I heard, and ended up moving in with her parents when Vince bailed on her. I think she named the boy Marc or Marcus or something."

Kara frowned and picked up her pen. "When was this?"

"Ah hell," Mac sighed, leaning back in his chair. He rested his cuffed hands in his lap. "I'm an old man now. This all happened when I was twenty-five, so forty-ish years ago?"

Kara nodded and wrote the year down. "And what was the woman's name?" she asked.

"Why does that matter?" Mac grumbled.

She looked up from her pad to level her gaze at him.

"Carlita Candela," Mac finally answered when he realized she wasn't budging.

Kara paused momentarily before she had to call on every fucking ounce of her courtroom etiquette to not freeze at hearing her mother's name. She wrote down her name and continued. "So, you were dating Carlita forty years ago. She cheated on you with your good friend Vince?" Kara prompted.

"Yes. I mean, she was a stripper and I should have expected that. But I loved her, you know?" Mac grumbled. "She was special."

Kara was dumbfounded. Absolutely dumbfounded. "How do you know the baby wasn't yours?" she finally asked.

Mac huffed a sigh. "I asked her about it. She said that Vince had wondered the same and wanted a paternity test done. She showed me the papers."

Kara nodded thoughtfully and continued. "So that was the end of your friendship with Vince?"

"Pretty much as soon as I walked in on them we had it out. Fistfight in the barracks. Both of us almost court-martialed. That was the end of it. Later, when she found out she was pregnant and didn't know whose it was, Vince pushed for the paternity test. The results just pretty much drove it home."

Kara could only nod as she watched him. There was nothing she could say to really add to it, so she remained silent.

Mac continued speaking, though, without needing to be encouraged. "At the time, Vince and I were months away from being discharged. We were going to go into business together. Case Holdings Ltd. was going to be our parent company. He was going into law; I was going to start a construction company. We had thought that by using the parent company, we could expand our brand. I dunno, it was a load of bullshit back then. I had filed for the tax ID and business license and had registered the business with the secretary of state already. Everything was ready for when we got discharged from the Marines. Then the shit happened with Lita..." he trailed off. "I forgot all about the business. Started the Ravager Knights with another buddy and eventually Taylor Construction and Mechanical. I forgot all about Case Holdings."

"Did Vince have the paperwork for Case Holdings?" Danvers finally spoke up, interjecting into the conversation.

"He must have. I never found it again," Mac said.

Danvers immediately turned to Kara. "Can you search your father's things?"

Kara immediately shook her head. "His house is covered in cameras, inside and out. It's more secure than Fort Knox, and he doesn't keep anything there. It's a museum practically. And he barely lives there anymore. He's been in the Caribbean for the last year with wife number four or five."

Danvers narrowed his eyes. "And his office at the Carmichael building?"

Again, Kara shook her head. "He cleared it out when he retired last year. Anything of importance would have gone to the archives for cases, and we only keep things on hand for ten years. After that, they go to an off-site document storage."

"That's convenient," Danvers rolled his eyes.

"I could try going through our files in the basement for something. Short of calling back every box that was ever sent off-site, there's not much more I can try. I run into dead en—"

"Do it," Danvers said.

"Do what?"

"Call back the boxes," he elaborated.

"Do you know how many fucking boxes that'll be? Thirty fucking years' worth of cases," Kara glared.

"Twenty, really." Danvers shrugged. He continued when he took in her confusion. "You said it yourself. You only keep ten years' worth of files on-site. Carmichael and Associates has been in business for the last thirty years. So call back those twenty years' worth of files. I'd bet money that you don't even have to. You'd probably find everything you need in the first years' worth of boxes."

Kara's mouth dropped open slightly as she stared at Danvers. "OK," she agreed.

Danvers smirked and nodded. "Now we're getting somewhere."

"You'll do it?" Mac asked, looking at her. "Go against your father?"

Kara hedged the question and answered in a roundabout way. "I'll order the boxes back and see what I can find regarding Case Holdings," she answered.

Mac grinned brightly. "That's good enough for me."

Kara smiled. "Sounds like a plan. Is there anything you want to add? Anything that happened over the years? Any contact with Vince?"

Mac shook his head. "After Lita confirmed Vince was the father, I never saw him again. I ran into Lita a couple years after that. The little boy looked more like her than Vince, but you could see it in him. His eyes were Vince's."

Kara nodded slowly. "I'm sorry that happened."

Mac shrugged. "I never thought about it again until I was picked up for this bullshit."

"We've got a good lead," Danvers assured him. "We'll get to the bottom of this."

"In the meantime, I'll look over everything that Danvers has and we'll get your defense going. We'll have to name my father to bring him in. That could get messy if I'm on counsel. Danvers will be primary and I'll help from the background. I won't be able to get involved publicly." Kara sighed.

Mac nodded. "Whatever you can do to help, I appreciate it."

Kara smiled wryly. "I can only do so much, but I don't see why we can't have hope."

Kara headed back to the office after she left the county jail. She swung by a sushi joint on her way and picked up lunch. She texted the group chat that something had come up at work and she would be working late, cancelling their plans for dinner.

She knew once she started digging she would lose track of time, and she didn't want to have to worry about being late for dinner with Johnny. He had wanted to take her on a date, just the two of them, to catch up on her day with his dad and then to get to know each other better. She had thought it was extremely sweet, but after learning the bombshell that Mac had dropped during the interview regarding her mother... she needed some alone time to process.

What would have happened if Carlita hadn't cheated on Mac? Would Kara still be here? Would Mac be her father? Johnny her brother? The what-ifs would drive her crazy, so she pushed them to the back of her mind.

She ate her sushi in her office and placed a call to the off-site document storage facility and ordered back every single box they ever sent. The woman she spoke to had been utterly shocked, but Kara had insisted. She gave them an address for a warehouse that Kara herself owned but rarely used. She would have the boxes delivered off-site so as not to raise suspicion from anyone in the office. She still didn't know whom she could trust and who was loyal to her father.

The lady had warned her it would take several weeks to organize a move that massive, as there were thousands of boxes, but Kara had assured her it was fine. She didn't have much of a choice but to wait.

Once that was organized, she started digging into the Granger files on her computer. She pulled up the billables and got lost in the financials. Case Holdings showed up multiple times but only as a charge for research.

Hours later, after hitting brick wall after brick wall, she called it quits.

Case Holdings was still as much of a mystery as it was that morning. Sure, she might now know who initially started the company. But how was her father using it now? Was he embezzling money from his own clients? From his own company?

Kara sighed when she finally logged out that evening. There really was only one way of knowing… and that was to ask her father outright.

Therein lay the problem. She and her father had a rocky relationship at best. They had worked well together when Vince was still in the office as long as she followed his lead. He was all for her making a name for herself and being ambitious, but it had to also be for the good of Carmichael and Associates as a whole.

They often fought over pro bono work and her volunteering at free legal clinics. She tried to give back to the community as much as she could. And while Vince loved the good publicity for the firm, he preferred her to be paid for her efforts and often tried to squash any attempts at her seeking too much pro bono work. Since his retirement, she hadn't had the time either—probably another idea of his.

She glanced at her phone and saw it was going on seven. Kara gathered up her purse and briefcase, with her laptop in tow, and headed for the door. Since it was Friday night, she decided to swing by the clubhouse, and see what her boys were up to. Maybe they could get a late dinner and head back to her place for some much-needed relaxation.

The clubhouse was more packed than Kara had ever seen it. There wasn't a place to park, so she pulled up in front of the row of bikes. Vagabond was sitting at the picnic tables beyond the bikes, so she headed his way.

"Hey, doll," he greeted her with a smile. "You staying a while? I can get one of the prospects to park your car out back."

"I'm not planning on it. Just passing through. What's the occasion?" she asked, motioning around at the extra people.

Vagabond grinned brightly. "Fight night. We're ordering the fight later and everyone is here to party and watch it. Fight starts at midnight our time, ten p.m. in Vegas."

Kara grinned. "Sounds fun. Have you seen Johnny or Derrick or Kevin?" she asked.

"'Round the pool table, last time I saw them," he nodded toward the clubhouse.

She grinned and headed that way. "Thanks Vagabond!"

She entered the smoky clubhouse and was taken by how packed it truly was. The music pumped through the speakers as scantily clad bodies writhed on a makeshift dance floor. The bar was packed two deep, while each booth and table were also full. The pool tables and dartboards had people hanging around, and Kara could barely make out her boys near one pool table at the back of the room.

She walked along the bar. Dressed in her work clothes and with her hair still up in a fancy chignon, she looked as out of place as she possibly could.

Kara didn't realize just how tired she was until a headache sprang up between her eyes and seemed to pulse with the heavy beat of the music.

She was almost at the back of the room when a woman wearing a bikini top and miniskirt that barely covered her ass stepped away from the bar. She looked Kara up and down and laughed. "Honey, you're gonna need to lose some clothes if you wanna hook up with anyone in this place."

Kara smiled easily and shrugged. "I'll take my chances," she said and pushed past the woman.

She got held up at the end of the bar when a girl fell off a barstool in front of her. Kara hadn't been close enough to reach her, but she had to wait to pass while a group of people helped the woman back up.

While she waited, she overheard a couple girls talking at the bar. "Have you tried talking to Mayhem tonight?" one asked.

Kara didn't turn to see the women. She didn't care who they were, but she listened. "I tried walking over there while they were playing pool. He told me he was busy and walked away. I figured I would try again later. I'm sure he'll need some relieving before the night is over."

The friend laughed. "Yeah, or not," she said. "I heard he's dating some lawyer."

"No way!" the first girl exclaimed. "But I heard that Devil, Rockstar, and Mayhem only date *together*, if you know what I mean."

The friend laughed again. "I know exactly what you mean. Whoever the lawyer is, she's lucky as hell."

Kara grinned to herself and continued on. With the crowd blocking her way gone, she had a clear path to her men. Johnny was bent over the table, lining up a shot and facing her, when he looked up and noticed her.

The grin that spread across his face sent her heart racing. He stood up and laid his pool cue down in the middle of the table as she walked up to him. "Beautiful, Princess," he greeted her and pulled her toward him when she was in arm's reach.

She smiled and let him pull her into his arms. He cradled her head between his hands, tilted her face, and leaned down to kiss her. She closed her eyes, wrapped her arms around his neck, and opened her mouth to meet his tongue. He tasted of whisky and nicotine. She knew he only smoked when he was stressed, so she ignored it and let him kiss her like she was his salvation.

When they pulled apart, breathless, she looked up at him with a dazed smile on her face. "Hi," she greeted.

"Hi." He grinned. "How'd it go with my dad?"

"It was enlightening. I've got some leads to follow and told Danvers I would work with him. Your father had a lot to say that was helpful. I think we have a real shot here," she answered honestly.

"Fuck yeah!" Johnny shouted loudly, causing most of the room to look over in confusion. Johnny grinned broadly as he picked her up by her waist and spun her around. She didn't have a choice but to wrap her legs around him.

She looked over his head to see Kevin and Derrick watching with their own happy grins. She looked back at Johnny just in time for him to lower her to the pool table and kiss her soundly again.

She laughed into the kiss and gave in, letting him have his way with her mouth.

"Let's go upstairs," he growled against her mouth.

She shook her head.

He paused and pulled back, looking confused. "What's wrong?" he asked, taking in her tired smile.

"Honestly, my head is killing me. It's been a really long day. I haven't eaten dinner yet. I just want to pick up some takeout on the way home, eat, maybe take a bath." She sighed, rubbing his face.

He frowned and rubbed her cheekbone with his thumb. "Add a couple orgasms to that list, and we'll get you feeling better in no time."

Kara laughed in disbelief. "But you have a clubhouse full of people here," she said, glancing around. She noticed some girls at the bar watching her with Johnny.

Kevin stepped up next to Johnny at the pool table and pulled her face toward his. "Not a problem, babe. Everyone can manage without us." He grinned and pressed a kiss to her mouth.

She moaned as his tongue tangled with hers. She groaned when Derrick's full beard tickled her neck as he placed an open-mouthed kiss to that sensitive spot he always homed in on. She sighed when Kevin broke the kiss. "I missed you guys today."

Johnny gave her a wicked grin. "Let us take care of you tonight."

She nodded slowly.

"You're gonna be so boneless by the end of the night you won't feel pain anywhere in that pretty body," Derrick murmured in her ear.

# Chapter Fourteen

Rockstar stood with Johnny in the compound lot, watching Kara drive away, Devil following her on his bike. "You really OK with leaving with a houseful?" Kevin asked, skeptically.

Johnny shook his head. "Not really." He sighed. "She just... I dunno man. She gets under my skin and makes me do things I'd never do for anyone else."

Kevin smirked. "Sounds like you love her."

Johnny snapped his gaze to Kevin, glaring. But oddly enough, he didn't say anything. "Fuck you," he settled on.

Kevin laughed and patted Johnny's shoulder. "Nah, let's talk to Mammoth and Hotrod about us disappearing for the evening. Let them know they're in charge so we can go fuck our girl."

Johnny smirked. He was still getting used to that. *Our girl.* It was all so new still, and he found that he was loving every minute of it. "Yeah, brother. Let's get out of here."

It didn't take long to grab Hotrod and Mammoth and pull them into church. Johnny and Kevin explained the situation and took the well-earned ribbing that both men threw their way. "Oh, leaving for some pussy?" "Not enough pussy here for you two? Gotta share the same one?"

Johnny grinned and bore it. Not many people understood how he could share everything with Derrick and Kevin, especially a woman. It just came naturally to them. After a decade in the Marines together, they were used to sharing everything and to sleeping next to each other on the ground, sharing body heat. Johnny often woke up in the middle of the night and reached out for his brother, to make sure he was still alive, only to find empty air.

After waking up in the middle of the night one too many times and reaching out for a brother only to startle the woman who'd shared his bed, Johnny had brought it up to his brothers. While they hadn't talked about it, Johnny had heard his brothers shout out in their sleep in the middle of the night as well.

Both Kevin and Derrick had looked relieved when he broached the topic of sharing, as if they had been thinking the same thing. Now, on nights they didn't have a woman between them, they often fell into the same bed together when the nightmares became too heavy. They were brothers in every sense of the word and leaned on each other when needed.

Once the meeting with Mammoth and Hotrod was done, they left the clubhouse quickly, not wanting to get sucked into another conversation and leave Kara alone with Derrick for too long. Johnny was alright sharing with his brothers to a point. Then he needed to join in too.

The ride to the west side was peaceful. Traffic had tapered off from the rush hour madness of a Friday night. Kara's house was twenty minutes from the clubhouse and nestled into an older neighborhood with deep lots and old trees. It was one of those neighborhoods that was starting to tear down the older, smaller homes to build McMansions on the large lots.

Kara's home had surprised him the first time he saw it. It was a new, modern Craftsman with four bedrooms and a two-car garage, but compared to the McMansions in the neighborhood, it was modest and small.

He and Kevin pulled in the driveway and into the open garage. They parked next to Derrick's motorcycle and shut off their bikes. With any luck, their boy would have her already relaxed and ready for a couple orgasms.

Kara groaned as Derrick's fingers worked magic on her sore neck and shoulders. The bathwater was warm around them. She leaned against his naked chest and sighed. Her eyes closed, she let him manipulate her muscles into submission.

Her tummy growled and she grumbled. "I'm starving, but I don't want you to stop."

There was a knock on the bathroom door before it was pushed open. She cracked her eyes to see Johnny and Kevin walk in the master bathroom. "Fucking beautiful, Princess," Johnny murmured.

She grinned and closed her eyes again, not caring that she was completely naked and on display for them. "How you doing, baby?" Kevin's voice was soft and closer to her.

"Hungry," she murmured.

A hand dipped below the water and slid along her thigh. "Hungry, huh?" Kevin chuckled. "Hungry for what?"

"Food," she replied instantly. "Real food. Pizza."

Kevin chuckled and slid his hand up her thigh to her core. Derrick grabbed her other thigh and pulled her legs further apart. Kevin's fingers slid into her cunt and she moaned softly. She peeked to see Kevin's dark eyes close to hers. He had crouched down next to the tub to lean over the water.

Behind him, Johnny leaned back against the vanity, arms crossed over his chest as he watched her. The leather of his cut pulled across his chest.

Kevin twisted his fingers in her cunt and she gasped, her eyes flashing to his dark orbs.

Derrick slid his hands up her belly and ribs. He cupped her breasts and kneaded them. His fingers pinched her nipples and she groaned. Her eyes slid closed and she lost herself in the sensations. She felt weightless in the water. "What a beautiful whore." Johnny's voice was deep and sensual from across the bathroom.

She smiled and sighed as Derrick's hands slid up her chest and around her shoulders. Kevin's fingers in her pussy curled forward against her G-spot. She arched as his thumb circled her clit. One of Derrick's arms wrapped around her ribcage and held her in place while Kevin increased his tempo.

She writhed on Derrick's lap as much as he'd let her, water splashing gently. His other hand went to work on one of her tits, pinching down on a nipple as Kevin twisted her clit. "Come for me," Johnny commanded from the vanity.

Kara moaned and threw her head back against Derrick's shoulder as her orgasm rolled over her. Her body shuddered and shook as Kevin worked her pussy. "Good girl," Kevin said before he gripped her jaw and kissed her roughly.

A while later, Kara was snuggled in her robe on the couch between Johnny and Kevin. She hadn't bothered getting dressed after the bath. Pizza had been delivered, and they were relaxing while watching an action movie. "You guys really don't have to stay with me," Kara said, eyes on the TV. "I know you have that big fight you want to watch. I'm honestly just gonna pass out soon. My head's feeling better."

A hand came up on the back of her neck and squeezed. She jumped at the pressure but found she could not turn around. "Little whore," Johnny growled in her ear. "Don't presume to know where I'd rather be."

Her heart skipped a beat and she flushed. "Safe words, Kara?" Kevin asked.

"Red for stop, yellow to slow down, and green for good," she answered immediately.

"Good girl," Kevin responded.

"On your knees," Johnny said, pushing her forward.

She went easily and let him guide her between his sprawled legs. He tossed a throw pillow on the floor between his feet and she slowly knelt before him, knees on the pillow. Johnny reached for her plate on the coffee table and set it on the cushion next to him. Kara settled between his legs and waited.

He lifted her piece of pizza to her mouth and she took a tentative bite, her eyes on his. "Eat," he nodded.

She settled further back onto her legs and rested her hands in her lap. She lowered her eyes and let her world narrow down to just the feel of the pillow beneath her knees and the soft material of her robe beneath her hands. She ate her pizza slowly and closed her eyes. She focused on the tastes and the textures.

The cheese, the marinara and spices, the sausage and pepperoni. It tasted like heaven in her mouth. She only opened her eyes to take another bite and then let the world fade away again. When she was done eating, Johnny pressed the straw from her water cup to her lips, and she took several deep draws.

After she had all the water she wanted, Johnny offered her more pizza, silently holding up a new slice. When she shook her head, he moved the pizza to the side and gripped the back of her head. She let him position her head on his thigh and closed her eyes when he started petting her hair

This was new territory for her. Petting and kneeling. She didn't know what to do with herself. No one had ever *taken care* of her before, not as an adult. She felt overwhelmed. Her eyes snapped open as her chest started to constrict and her breathing grew labored.

"Breathe," Johnny ordered, his voice deep. His hand gripped the back of her neck with a heavy pressure, but it didn't hurt. She found it grounded her.

She closed her eyes again and slid her hands up his legs. One arm wrapped around his back while the other slipped under his shirt to find skin. Only when her hand was flat on his abdomen, his skin soft and warm beneath her fingers, did she finally calm down.

She focused on her breathing and the feel of the warm, soft skin of Johnny's belly beneath her hand. The rough but worn denim against her face, beneath her cheek. The heavy hand, covered in calluses on the back of her neck, holding her in place. The soft chenille pillow beneath her bare knees.

She let her world only consist of the things she could touch, feel, smell. Johnny's leather and sandalwood. The heat of his body. Her mind emptied of all thoughts as she narrowed her world down. A deep sigh left her lips as she melted against his leg, feeling boneless.

"Good girl," he whispered, so softly.

Her head grew fuzzy, and all sounds drifted away.

She didn't know if she fell asleep. She had never felt anything like this before. A tranquility. A space between time and thought. She nuzzled against Johnny's thigh and rubbed his abs with her hand. He was soft and hard and rough at the same time.

"Such a good girl," his voice was soft and far away. "Kneeling for me, like the pretty Princess you are," he continued. "So beautiful."

When Kara stopped moving and it was clear that she had fallen asleep and was not just in subspace, Johnny sighed and started petting her hair, mindlessly. "We should move her to bed," he said, not looking away from her.

"Have you done this before?" Derrick asked. "I've read about subspace, but I've never had anyone submit to me quite like Kara just did."

Johnny shook his head. "No, just read about it."

"We need to be careful," Kevin said. "She trusted you to go under, then fell asleep. She could experience sub drop while sleeping. You should probably be the first thing she sees when she wakes up, just in case."

Johnny nodded, already knowing that but grateful to hear it confirmed. Sub drop could happen to anyone after an emotional scene, and while they hadn't played any differently than normal, he had made her kneel for him as he fed her. He had watched the panic well up in her before he calmed her down. Was it enough of an emotional upheaval to trigger a drop? He didn't know, but he also wasn't willing to chance anything. Not with her.

He reached down and arranged her arms before he slid his own arms around her and under her knees. He managed to gather her up on his lap and stopped a moment.

With her head on his shoulder, her face clean of all makeup and relaxed from all worry, she looked ten years younger than her thirty years. Not that she looked old for her age at all, but she carried the weight of the world on her shoulders.

His heart pounded in his chest as he thought of how she had *trusted* him. How she had *leaned into him.* How easily she had accepted the three of them. He brushed back her hair from her face and pressed a gentle kiss to her lips.

His brothers thankfully didn't utter a word as he stared down at the blond beauty. He'd never felt like this before with *anyone.* When he told his father she was special, he had meant it.

"She really is amazing," Derrick murmured behind him.

Johnny looked back over his shoulder to see Derrick and Kevin gazing down at her with matching looks of reverence on their faces. "I told you guys," Kevin said softly.

Once they had carefully placed a naked Kara in the center of her large bed, Johnny climbed into her shower for a quick wash. He didn't want to dirty her bed after a day of work. Johnny had a feeling he was falling in love with the blond-haired, blue-eyed beauty in the other room.

He knew Kevin was already there, had been there since the beginning, but he had a feeling Derrick was feeling it too. They were all so thoroughly *fucked*.

Johnny didn't waste time in the shower. He quickly washed up with her fancy as fuck bodywash and vowed that the next time he hit the store, he'd pick up his own shit for her place. They spent enough time there.

He should think about bringing her by their place too.

Once he dried off, he put his boxers back on and thought about leaving some clothes at her place, too, before he headed back out to her bedroom. Derrick and Kevin were sitting at the end of the bed watching her. Neither had taken off their clothes or showered. They were clearly waiting for their turns.

Derrick got up and headed for the bathroom as Johnny slid into Kara's bed beside her. It was early still, just after nine o'clock, but Kara had a long day on top of a long week, and Johnny was feeling it too. He slid in next to her and wrapped his arms around her. He pressed a kiss to her forehead and pulled the covers up around them.

"You love her," Kevin stated softly.

"Yeah," Johnny answered without hesitating.

"Good." Kevin nodded.

Johnny didn't reply, just watched her and rubbed her back, ran his hand over her arm, touched the skin of her ribs and belly. He couldn't stop touching her and staring. She was beautiful and so, so soft.

Eventually he drifted off to sleep. Someone had turned off her bedroom lights but left on the light in the bathroom and cracked the door to let in some light. Kara shifted in his arms and let out a little cry.

Johnny was instantly on alert. "It's alright, Princess. I've got you," he murmured.

"Johnny?" she asked, her voice thick with sleep.

"Right here, Princess," he said and pulled her closer.

She wrapped her arm around his waist and buried her face in his chest. He could feel the tears wetting his skin.

"You're alright. We're right here," he said.

"Derrick? Kevin?" she asked.

"Right here, baby girl," Derrick's voice was also thick with sleep. Johnny felt Derrick's hand reach out and run down her back, sliding across Johnny's arm in the process.

"Me too, babe," Kevin said from the other side of Derrick.

She reached back and laced her fingers together with Kevin's, pulling his hand toward her. "I don't know why I'm crying," she sighed.

"It's likely sub drop," Johnny spoke softly, rubbing her back. "You went into subspace so easily and then fell asleep. You're alright, we've got you."

She shifted in his arms and peered up at him. Her hand slid over his jaw, her fingers combing through the blond beard that was growing longer than he usually let it. She seemed to like it, so he hadn't trimmed. She pressed a kiss to his lips before she licked into his mouth.

He flicked his tongue against hers but otherwise let her lead the kiss. Derrick's hands slid between them and cupped her breasts. She moaned into Johnny's mouth and bit down on his lower lip.

He groaned and tightened his hold on her as she sucked his lower lip into her mouth. God, it felt fantastic. She broke the kiss a moment later, panting and breathless. She turned her head to Derrick, and he grabbed her jaw and kissed her passionately.

Kara sighed into the kiss. Derrick worked his tongue against hers, his mouth moving against hers so sensually. Her pussy throbbed. Desperation sparked inside of her as he squeezed her breasts roughly.

For as sweet and as soft as Johnny had been, Derrick was now the aggressive one. Her dazed and confused brain was struggling to keep up and yet on board with it all at the same time. She wanted him to take charge, wanted to mount him too. "Derrick," she groaned against his lips.

"Come 'ere, baby," he growled, flipping onto his back and pulling her on top of him at the same time. She straddled his waist and gasped when her naked core landed on his bare dick.

She braced herself with her hands on his chest and waited. The room was dimly lit, the only light from the cracked bathroom door. She reached between her and Derrick and grabbed his cock, lining him up with her opening and slowly sinking down on him. She was wet and ready, but his girth always had her pausing. All three of her men were large, and her body needed a minute to adjust.

Derrick's hands were on her hips, and he quickly took over. He lifted her up and slammed her down without warning. She cried out and gripped his wrists. All she could do was hold on while he took charge.

Hands cupped her breasts before the scrape of a beard kissed along her neck. She leaned back and rested her head against Johnny's shoulder as he mouthed kisses into the sweet spot of her neck. She reached up and cupped his face and pressed him harder into her neck. He took the hint and sucked down hard on the sensitive skin. She moaned and panted. She tried to buck her hips, but Derrick's grip on her hips was too strong.

Johnny pinched her nipples and she gasped again.

Her eyes flew open when another hand snaked between her and Derrick's bodies and circled her clit, rubbing her. She watched Kevin hand Johnny a bottle of lube at the same time as his fingers toyed with her clit.

It was the hottest thing she'd seen in a while. She groaned and reached for Kevin. She wrapped her hand around his neck and pulled him toward her by the nape of his neck. He cupped her jaw and kissed her.

She moaned into the kiss as Johnny slipped a lube-covered finger into her ass. Her emotions were all over the place. She gave up on the kiss with Kevin, panting. She let her head fall forward onto his shoulder.

He pressed a kiss to her forehead and ran a hand over her hair. "So good for us, Kara," he murmured.

She slid her hand down his bare chest, marveling at the muscles, before she found his happy trail. She followed the trimmed hair down to his hard cock and wrapped her fingers around the base.

A heavy hand came down between her shoulder blades and pushed her down. Derrick pulled her in for kiss before a hand fisted in her hair and her head was yanked toward Kevin's dick. She groaned as she wrapped her lips around him as Johnny popped the head of his cock into her ass.

Derrick stopped moving to let Johnny in, and Kevin took advantage of her gasp to slide deeper into her mouth. She let herself go, let her guys take charge and use her body. She let them set the pace and only focused on the pleasure her body received. Kevin fucked her throat, and she barely did more than hold open her mouth as he fucked her face, using the hand fisted in her hair to guide her.

Johnny and Derrick found a rhythm in her ass and cunt. She was a moaning, sobbing mess when she came violently. A moment later, her body shook among the three cocks pummeling her, but they didn't slow down. They didn't stop.

This time when that floaty feeling overcame her and she felt like every nerve ending was electrified and she could feel every thread beneath her knees, she recognized the feeling for what it was: *subspace.*

She threw herself into the feeling head-on and cried out as she came again, the orgasm far more intense than ever before.

When she came to, she was sitting up, cradled with her back against a strong chest. Hands rubbed up and down her arms, over her thighs, and across her belly. She was still on top of Derrick. She squeezed the muscles of her pussy around his cock, and he groaned low.

"There's the pretty, Princess," Johnny said softly. The hands stroking up and down her arms slid up to her face and gently turned it to look back over her shoulder. Johnny was still in her ass, still hard.

"Mmmm," she murmured and snuggled into his neck, enjoying the feeling of his beard against her skin.

"How you doing, babe?" Kevin asked softly. His voice sounded far away.

She shifted in Johnny's hold to peer over at Kevin, who was sitting at the edge of the bed, his cock still hard. She smiled lazily at him when she met his gaze. She still felt floaty and nonverbal. The thought of words was too much effort for her. She reached out a hand to him and he laced their fingers together.

She closed her eyes again and let the feeling of being full wash over her. She opened her eyes when Kevin pulled his hand away. She watched him reach over to the nightstand and pick up her blue and green insulated water cup. He turned back to her and raised the straw to her lips.

She took a slow sip and enjoyed the cool water easing her throat. She took another sip and leaned back against Johnny when she was done. Kevin put the cup back on the nightstand and then moved toward her again.

"Ready?" Derrick asked and rolled his hips.

She gasped and nodded. She licked her lips and eyed Kevin's cock. He grinned and moved toward her. Once he was kneeling within reach, she bent toward him and licked the head of his cock, flicking her tongue against the sensitive flesh. He groaned when she swirled her tongue over him.

She slowly sucked him into her mouth as Johnny and Derrick started moving inside her. She whimpered around Kevin's cock and reached out to grab the base of it. A hand clamped down on her wrist a moment later and her hand was twisted behind her back.

"Uh-uh, whore. You use your mouth only," Johnny said.

Shivers ran down her spine as he reached out and secured both hands behind her back. She keened loudly around Kevin's cock as Johnny and Derrick picked up their pace. Kevin held her face with both hands and fucked her mouth.

She lost herself in the punishing pace the three of them set. She moaned as her orgasm rolled over her. "Fuck, babe," Kevin groaned before he bottomed out in her throat and his body shuddered as he came. She only got a faint taste of him as he pulled out. "So good for us, baby." He pushed her hair out of her face and rubbed his thumb along her cheekbone.

Derrick's fingers tightened on her hips and he pulled her down tight, his cock buried to the hilt. "Fucking hell, baby girl," he groaned as he shot his load deep inside her.

Johnny followed a moment later, squeezing her wrists tighter as his hips pounding her ass stuttered to a halt. "Princess, fuuuuccck," he groaned.

Kara pulled her arms back around her and steadied herself over Derrick. He grinned wickedly at her and pulled her down for a breathtaking kiss.

"So fucking perfect, Kara," Johnny groaned and kissed up her spine before he slowly pulled out.

A shiver racked her at the loss of body heat. Kevin immediately reached for the blankets at the foot of the massive bed and tossed them over her and Derrick. She smiled gratefully and nuzzled into the crook of Derrick's neck. She smoothed his thick beard out of her face and closed her eyes as she caught her breath.

"How you doing, baby girl?" Derrick asked softly.

"Mmm," she moaned, a content smile on her face. "So good. So fucking good," she drawled.

Derrick's laugh rumbled through his chest and hers.

She grinned and slowly eased off his softening cock. She was sore and exhausted and it was still the middle of the night judging by the dark windows. "I need a shower." She sighed. "My hair's a mess."

"Looks sexy." Kevin grinned from across the bed where he was sliding back into his boxers.

Kara rolled her eyes and eased out of bed. She headed into the bathroom, where Johnny had started the shower and was currently inside the glass enclosure washing off. She smiled and climbed in with him. "Hi," she murmured as she stepped toward him under the warm spray of the waterfall showerhead.

He smiled easily. "Hey, Princess."

She leaned up for a kiss and sighed as the warm water cascaded down her back.

"You want help?" Johnny asked.

She opened her eyes and shook her head. "I'm OK."

He placed another kiss to her lips, then turned and got out of the shower.

She closed her eyes again and let the water calm her racing heart.

# Chapter Fifteen

T HE NEXT MORNING KARA woke to the smell of bacon cooking. She yawned and stretched in bed, listening to her spine pop as it realigned. "That's fucking creepy." Kevin chuckled from next to her.

She grinned and rolled to face him. "Hi, sexy."

"Hi, beautiful." He wrapped his arm around her and pulled her closer.

"Where is everyone?" she asked, rubbing her hand over his bare back.

"Derrick is cooking, so probably making a mess of your kitchen." Kevin chuckled.

She giggled and shrugged, not too worried about it.

"And Johnny ran to the clubhouse for a couple hours this morning. Wanted to check in on the cleaning process and grab some of his shit."

"Like his bodywash?" She laughed.

"Absolutely. About time too. If I have to hear him grumble about girly scents one more time…" Kevin laughed.

She giggled and pressed a kiss to the underside of Kevin's jaw. "Is he grabbing your stuff too?"

"Yeah, some clothes and shit for me and Derrick." Kevin nodded. "You OK with that?"

She nodded and smiled. "I am OK with all of that."

"This doesn't seem fast to you?" he clarified, raising an eyebrow at her.

She paused and frowned slightly. She looked up at him and rubbed a hand over his day's old stubble. "I—no, I'm OK with how we've been moving. It may have been a little quick, but I'm comfortable with where we're at now," she admitted.

Kevin cupped her jaw between his thumb and forefinger and tilted her head up to kiss her. The kiss was slow and sensual, a sweet kiss from a man she had quickly fallen in love with. She opened her mouth slowly and let the kiss turn more passionate.

Kevin rolled over onto her, and she shifted so he was cradled between her open thighs. He rested his weight on his forearms, bracing on either side of her head while he continued to kiss her.

She ran her hands down his bare back to his boxer-clad ass, slipping her hands under the hem and skated one along his hip to his front. Wrapping her hand around his cock, he moaned into the kiss while he bucked into her palm.

She made quick work of pulling off his boxers and kicking them out of the way. She moaned as he slid inside her slowly. "Fuck, Kevin." She groaned against his mouth.

"That's how you make me feel, babe. Every time. You feel fucking amazing." He panted as he rocked gently against her.

Their lovemaking was slow and sensual, because that's what it was—making love. They were unhurried and lazy, a stark contrast to the past couple weeks with her men.

"Kevin." She moaned and arched her back as he hit the spot right where she liked it.

He put a bruising kiss on her neck and sucked down, biting her gently.

She shattered around him and moaned loudly.

"That's it, my beautiful love," he murmured and increased his pace. "Fuck, Kara." He groaned when he came soon after.

He collapsed onto her and she smiled, wrapping her arms around him as she accepted his weight. She loved every inch of him pressed against her. She closed her eyes and savored the feeling. She kept her mouth closed, not knowing what might come out of it if she spoke.

When he shifted and some of his weight lifted off her, she opened her eyes to see his warm chocolate orbs gazing down at her. There was such reverence and love within them she gasped. The emotion that was on his face was everything.

All she could do was stare back and wonder.

A knock to the open door startled her before Derrick asked, "You guys hungry?"

"Fuck off," Kevin shouted, looking over his shoulder to toss a pillow at Derrick.

Kara laughed and sighed. The moment was ruined, but she had felt it clearly. There were feelings there. He was feeling it too. She wasn't alone in her fall for him.

Kara spent the rest of the weekend in a blissed-out state. Her boys spent the time at her house, supplying her with orgasm after orgasm. She had never been so happy in her life or as satiated. They kept her well fed and relaxed in bed most of the weekend, watching movies when they weren't fucking her senseless.

Kara couldn't remember the last time she felt so relaxed. By the time Sunday evening came around, Kara felt like crying when her boys said they had to go. "You should get a good night's sleep before Monday," Kevin tried to reason. "And our charter from Cali will be here this evening. We need to be there to greet them, Johnny especially."

Kara pouted. "You really think I'll be able to sleep alone after one of you has been sleeping with me the last several weeks?" She raised an eyebrow at them. She understood they needed to leave; they had responsibilities. She would still miss them in her bed, though.

Johnny smirked and looked up from the boots he was lacing up. "Pretty pout on a pretty Princess," he commented.

"Would look prettier on a penis," she continued with a smirk of her own.

"Sure does," Johnny countered back immediately. "I'll just have to remember all the times I fucked those pretty lips until I can fuck them again."

Kara frowned. She didn't like they were making light of this. "Johnny." She leveled a stare at him, though she was sure it wasn't as effective as it could be because she felt tears welling in her eyes.

He frowned when he looked up at her. He stood up from the chair he'd been sitting in and reached for her. She went easily and buried her face in his chest. She didn't know why the thought of them leaving made her so upset. She'd never minded being alone before now.

She may have never realized just how *lonely* she had been before them, though. Or how empty her house felt when it was just her. She sniffled into his shirt, and he held her tighter. "Shh," he muttered. "It's not forever. We'll see you this week at the office." *God, he's just a giant teddy bear when he wants to be.*

The front door suddenly swung open and Derrick called out, "Yo Mayhem, Rockstar, we leaving?" His boots were heavy on her hardwood floors as he headed into the kitchen. "Oh shit," he muttered when he took in Kara in Johnny's arms.

Johnny's hand rubbed down her back.

"What's the matter, baby girl?" Derrick asked and moved closer.

Kara shrugged. She really didn't want to answer, afraid she would start sobbing. Tears ran silently down her cheeks, and she didn't know why she was so upset.

She just had a bad feeling in her chest that this would be the last time they would all be together like this.

She wiped her eyes and pulled away. She leaned up and pressed a kiss to the underside of Johnny's jaw, right in his beard. "Go, I'll see you guys this week," she said, sounding stronger than she felt. She gave Kevin and Derrick brief hugs, unable to meet their eyes, before she quickly left the kitchen and went back to her bedroom.

She didn't need to watch them leave.

She climbed under the messy sheets and blankets and buried her face into a pillow that smelled like Derrick. A few minutes later she heard the rumble of their Harleys start up. She let the tears fall as she prayed like hell that she was wrong about the feeling in her gut.

She wasn't usually wrong, though.

# Chapter Sixteen

Kara's week dragged. Monday had been horrible. She hadn't slept much the night before, despite how tired and sore she had been from her weekend of *extra-curricular activities*. She had been stuck in back-to-back meetings throughout the day and hadn't been able to check her phone.

So when she finally had a chance, she was extra disappointed by the lonely text from Kevin that explained they were hosting a fight at the clubhouse that night and would not be able to come by her place.

Annoyed by the single text and lack of invitation to join them at the clubhouse, she had fired off a quick **OK** and let it go.

The boys hadn't been on the jobsite all week, though their crew was still there. Derrick had texted the group chat on Tuesday to say they were tied up with their out-of-state guests and would not be in that week. There was no other explanation.

When she didn't hear from them that evening, she went to bed pissed off.

Wednesday she tried to brush off her bad mood. She reached out to their group chat to check in, in the morning. She sent a simple text: **"Morning, hope you guys have a wonderful day!"** It went unread and unanswered all day.

When she got home that night, she had to fight the tears as she ate dinner alone. She didn't understand why they weren't responding to her. She knew she wasn't being clingy, but she couldn't help but have doubts.

Doubts about all of it. After a weekend sex-a-thon, were they done with her? Did they have their fill, and were they ready to move on? Was she just another whore to them? The last one really got to her. They had never made her feel dirty while they were fucking her, but there had been no grand declarations of love either.

She'd had that moment with Kevin... That was another thing that bothered her. Kevin usually called her in the evenings to check in when he was away for club business. But there hadn't been a peep from him either.

That had hurt the most. She had started all of this by dating just him, not his brothers. Now she didn't know where she stood with any of them. She hated the self-conscious doubts that crept in, hated how the little girl deep inside her that just wanted to be loved showed her ugly head.

She forced down the feelings and the thoughts and decided to call her big brother. It had been too long since they'd had one of their talks, and she missed him.

She curled up on the couch in the great room and pressed her phone to her ear. *"Hola, mi estrella brillante"* (hello, my shining star). Marcos's deeply accented voice answered on the third ring. It was loud on his end, lots of shouting. She heard a door close before the sound was cut off.

"Hey, big brother," she greeted with a sigh.

"Oh no, *chaparrita* (shorty). I know that sigh," he groaned. "What happened? *A quien tengo que matar?*" (Who do I have to kill?)

She smiled sadly even though he couldn't see her. "Nah, it's not like that, *manito*. I'm just having a bad day."

He hummed noncommittedly. "What have you been up to?" he asked instead.

"I met someone," she started, wondering how to broach the subject of dating three men. She honestly didn't even know if she was dating them or if they were just fucking around at this point.

Marcos chuckled darkly. "Yeah, lil *manita*? He the reason you're calling me upset?"

Kara rolled her eyes. Maybe she shouldn't have called him after all. He could always read her, always catch her in a lie, even over the phone.

"No, Marquitos," she groaned. "I told you, I had a bad day. You gonna keep being an ass, or can I tell you about them?"

"Them?" He homed in on that word immediately.

Now Kara did groan. Her brother was ten years older than her and took after their mother more than she did. He was raised more Mexican while she had been raised more American. Even their last names were different: Marcos Candela and Kara Carmichael.

Their mother had claimed it was because she was born with blond hair and blue eyes that she had received their father's last name. Kara didn't question it because Marc hated talking about their father.

She hadn't even told him about her visit to Mac in county jail. There was a lot she hadn't told her brother about in the last two months. Their weekly text check-ins were lacking.

"Si, manito," she sighed and stood from the couch. She started pacing, figuring she might as well tell him. "Them. I'm dating three men at the same time."

"Pinche cabróns," (fucking bastards). Marcos growled. "The hell you are. No sister of mine will be some whore," he added in English. His tone immediately set her off, her own anger rising to the challenge.

"Well you better believe it, Marcos," she snapped. "Because I just spent all weekend with the three of them getting railed in every hole I've got, and I fucking loved it! So fuck you and your backward-ass thinking." She hung up the phone after that.

He didn't call back.

She finally gave in to her tears and went into her bedroom to bury herself under the covers as the sobs racked her body. She hated fighting with her brother, hated that she had to defend herself with him and put up with his chauvinistic bullshit all the time.

Some days he was more like their father than he knew.

The next morning, Kara woke to crusty and swollen eyes. She hadn't taken her makeup off before crying her eyes out all night. She had barely slept. Her throat hurt and her nose was stuffy. She sent her assistant a text that she wouldn't be coming into the office and crawled back to bed.

She managed to sleep for a couple more hours and felt a little better when she woke up. She rolled out of bed and hit the shower right away. It was after ten when she finished.

Her face was still slightly puffy from crying, but her sinuses were clear again. She knew her throat would be better once she had some water. She headed to the kitchen to find something to eat when she heard her phone ringing from the bedroom. She doubled back for her phone and groaned when she saw her father's name on the screen.

She thought about ignoring the call but knew he would just continue to blow up her phone until she answered him. "Good morning, Dad," she greeted pleasantly.

"Morning, daughter," he replied. Well that was good at least; it sounded like he was in a good mood.

"How can I help you this morning?" She headed for the kitchen with the phone pressed to her ear.

"Well, I'm wondering where you are. I'm at the office and you aren't here," he deadpanned.

Kara stopped dead in her living room. "You're in town?" she questioned.

"Sure am. Thought I would swing by the office and check on my darling daughter and see if she wanted to do lunch."

Kara's heart pounded in her chest. She hated when he sprung these surprise lunches or dinners on her. It usually meant he wanted something. It was how he delivered all his orders. "Well, I'm working from home today," she answered slowly, her mind racing. "I had a client dinner run late last night."

"Let's do dinner instead then. I have some things I wanted to do around the city anyway. How about Supérieur?" he suggested.

Kara rolled her eyes. "Sure, Dad. Sounds great."

"Great. I'll see you at seven," her father said before he hung up.

Kara shook her head in disbelief. This was turning out to be the week from absolute hell.

That evening, Kara was dressed in a modest navy-blue dress to meet her father at the stupid French restaurant men like him loved. Her hair was pulled back in a sleek ponytail, and she had a dusting of makeup on her face. She looked posh.

She hoped her father was still in a good mood when she arrived.

She parked her MKX in front of the valet stand and quickly handed off her keys. She hated valets most of the time. She would rather park her own vehicle and walk so that if she wanted to leave she could find it easily.

The doorman opened the door, and she quickly gave her name to the maître d'. Her father had a standing reservation at the all the fancy restaurants in Mourningside. Being his daughter had some benefits, she had to admit. Other times, it was more a nuisance.

Before the maître d' could reply, she saw her father across the room at his usual table. It was a large banquette that was on a raised platform along the back wall. It was really two tables, but they were both his. Most nights they were pushed together to form one large table, but tonight, thankfully, they were separated.

The banquette had a view of the entire dining area and a great view of the large, open window that allowed patrons to watch as the kitchen staff prepared their food.

It also let him feel like he lorded over all of them.

Kara hated it. The long banquette was too much for just the two of them. They would end up sitting side by side and facing the room instead of each other.

She would have to grin and bear it. These types of dinners had been common with her father ever since he "swooped in and saved her from state school," as he claimed. She had already been in her third year of college at Northern Illinois University and declared a prelaw degree when he had reached out, claiming he got her phone number from the school records.

Regardless, he had swept in and offered Harvard on a silver platter. At the time, she felt she would have been an idiot to turn down an offer of that magnitude. Despite Marcos's warnings of strings being attached, she accepted her father's offer and transferred to Harvard the second semester of her junior year. She finished out her undergrad and then went to Harvard Law School.

When she moved back to Mourningside, she discovered the strings that Marcos had warned her about. Instead of going to work at the nonprofit law clinic on the south side, helping kids like her and low-income families as she had dreamed of when she was in law school, she was given a job at Carmichael and Associates.

She refused to take the junior partner job her father had handed her, instead working her way up through the ranks as an associate until she became the youngest senior partner the firm had seen. It only made sense that when her father announced his retirement she would take over as managing partner.

Kara squared her shoulders and walked across the room. Her father's eyes swept over her attire quickly before he met her gaze and smiled. That was a good start, she supposed. Appearances were everything to him. "Hello, Dad," she greeted with a demure smile.

Her father stood from the other side of the banquette and walked between the two tables. He met her when she reached the top of the platform and greeted her with a smile and a kiss to her cheek. "Beautiful as ever, darling."

Vince Carmichael was as handsome and formidable as ever. Tall, with a lithe muscular build, he filled out his tailored, three-piece Hermes suit to perfection. At sixty-five, her father's blond hair had taken on a white-blond sheen that was very in right now. His blue eyes crinkled in the corners, but her father was still very attractive for his age.

Kara chose the seat across from him and sat with her back to the room.

He frowned slightly but otherwise didn't comment. "How was your day at home?"

Kara steeled her spine. "It was fine. I managed to catch up on my case files." She had, but it wasn't something she had planned on doing until after her father called.

He nodded absently as a sommelier walked over in a tuxedo. "Good evening, Lady, Gentleman," he greeted with a soft voice. "Can I interest you in our wine menu?"

"Yes," Vince answered and reached for the menu the man handed him, as if he didn't order the same fucking wine every time they came here. "Ah yes, we'll try the Domaine de la Romanee-Conti Richebourg Grand Cru, 2017," he ordered.

Kara's eyebrows rose at the name of the bottle that easily cost five thousand dollars. "Are we celebrating something?" she asked when the sommelier walked away.

"Can't a father just want to spoil his daughter once in a while?" her father deflected with a smile.

Kara forced a smile to her lips but felt that he could see right through her. Even a decade later, her father still set her on edge. She was always waiting for the other shoe to drop with him.

A moment later the sommelier returned with two glasses and the bottle of wine her father had ordered. He set down the glasses, before he opened the bottle. He poured a small splash of red wine into a glass before handing it to her father.

She watched Vince as he sniffed the wine. He tilted the glass gently and swirled the wine around inside the glass before he sniffed it again. Then he took a small sip. She watched him swish it around his mouth before finally swallowing it. "Yes, that will do. Two glasses please, and leave the bottle."

Kara fought the urge to roll her eyes at his dismissive attitude. The sommelier poured two glasses half full before he left the bottle on the table with the label facing them. "Shall I leave the cork?" the sommelier asked.

"Yes, please," Kara answered with a smile before her father could refuse.

The man nodded before he walked away, and Kara was left with the uncomfortable silence that generally settled between her and her father. Too much left unsaid after too many years of abandonment.

They made small talk and ordered their food, or rather her father ordered for her. The duck. Yuck. She didn't argue. She only hoped that the dinner would pass quickly so she could get back into her pj's and wallow in her self-pity again.

"How is the remodel going in the office?" her father asked, changing the subject.

She finally smiled, genuinely. "It's going great," she answered.

When she didn't elaborate, he raised an eyebrow. "That's good," he deadpanned.

Kara fought the urge to snort. Was it always this stilted with her father? Or was she just in a particularly bad mood? *Could be the fact that he's embezzling from his own company and framing Mac to do it.* The thought nagged in her head.

After their food had been delivered and they'd started eating, Kara decided she was over the farce that was their dinner. She boldly asked, "What is Case Holdings?"

Her father's smile was slow and sharklike. "You know, I'm glad you brought that up. There was something I wanted to speak to you about." He made a show of patting his mouth with his napkin and took his time.

There it was, she thought. The *real* reason for this dinner.

Kara braced herself.

"Case Holdings is the company that is embezzling from Granger Ltd.," her father stated, as if she didn't already know this. "Thomas Granger reached out directly. He said that his current attorney, Ken Laraway, had recently found himself unemployed and was wondering if there was a way that I could assist."

Kara used every bit of her courtroom mask to appear emotionless as she stared at her father. He took his time, dragging out her discomfort.

"Imagine my surprise when I found myself backed against a wall," he drawled.

*Backed really hard, I'm sure.*

"And as you well know, the bylaws indicate we cannot release findings of internal investigations regarding employee misconduct," he droned on.

She plastered a bored smile on her face. "Of course not." She nodded.

"But as the man had also attacked my own daughter, well you can imagine, I found that I was unable to keep my mouth shut," Vince finished.

Kara felt her heart plummet. Her stomach turned as she stared at her father. "I see," she answered slowly and reached for her wine glass. She took a sip to buy herself time to think. Because she really *did* see what was happening here. Every bad feeling she had felt over the past week since her guys left her home suddenly came to light, and she kicked herself for not seeing it sooner. She took another sip of her wine while her father's crystal blue eyes were locked on her.

"Tom was appalled, naturally."

"Naturally," Kara agreed, nodding robotically and setting down her glass. Her hands were sweating. Her heart raced. She forced herself to calm down before the roaring in her ears caused her to miss anything the shark before her might say.

"When he asked that I handle the case *personally*," he emphasized, speaking slowly, "who was I to deny him?"

Kara smiled wryly. "I wouldn't expect anything less." She nodded at her father.

His smile grew more genuine, less predatory. "So," he drawled, "you'll understand when I ask you, kindly, to stop digging into Case Holdings." He said it so matter-of-factly, so nonchalantly, that she almost missed the veiled threat to his words. He was an expert at laying out opponents in the courtroom. He could wind a story up, work up the jury, and then deliver the final blow with a few simple sentences.

Kara smiled demurely and reached for her wine again. "And what is your relationship with Mac Taylor?" she asked.

Vince frowned and sighed dramatically. "I suppose he told you his version of events, did he?"

She didn't even bother to ask how he knew she had visited Mac at the county jail. He had eyes and ears everywhere, even if he was supposedly retired. "He did," she answered with a nod.

"Ah hell," Vince groaned. The man was a good actor, she would give him that. "It must have been forty years ago by now. Ancient history, or so I thought," he admonished. "Your mother was working at a strip club, a real dive of a place, but it made her happy, so I allowed it," he continued.

Kara had to force herself to breathe. There was a reason they purposely did not speak of her mother in the years since she had passed. Her mother had been her whole world. She had been a hardworking woman from what Kara remembered. Whatever she had done before Kara, it wasn't her business.

"She met Mac one night when he came in with some of the guys from the barracks." He rolled his eyes. "From what she said, a lap dance led to a kiss that led to fucking in the bathroom. Six weeks later she came crying to me that she was pregnant." He rolled his eyes again.

She was getting really sick of his arrogance.

"I told her I would pay for a paternity test. If the child was mine, I would help her. She went to a clinic and tried to give me forged documents, framing me as the father." He shook his head in disbelief. "Luckily, she had gone to a clinic where a friend of mine worked," he continued his lies. "He gave me a copy of the real results. Marcos is Mac's son. My fiancée cheated on me with my ex–best friend and got pregnant with his child."

Kara was seething inside. She had to clamp down on her emotions. She threw up every wall she could in her mind so as not to show how utterly incensed she felt.

"She fed Mac the same bullshit papers that it was my child. But I had the truth. She didn't deny it when I confronted her. I told her I wouldn't raise someone else's bastard child and she should leave." He shrugged.

Kara shook her head in disappointment. "I don't know why I expected anything else," she said, resigned.

He narrowed his gaze on her. "I wouldn't expect you to understand how a woman can imprison a man like that, lie about the child being his. It's inconceivable."

"So Mac is Marcos's father?" she questioned, glancing away.

Vince eyed her and nodded, and then he dropped his last surprise of the evening. "Yes, your half brother shares the same father as your boyfriend."

Kara's eyes flashed back to her father's. Her heart hammered in her chest as it constricted.

"Oh yes, my darling daughter," he drawled, a sneer on his face. "I know all about how you've been whoring yourself to those three bikers. Like mother, like daughter after all."

"How fucking dare—"

"No, how dare *you*," he snapped, immediately cutting her off. "After everything I did for you. Pulled you out of the slums, gave you Harvard. You would dishonor me by being a biker whore?!"

Rage colored her vision red. "Fuck you," she spat.

Vince laughed cruelly. "No, daughter, you've already fucked half the town."

She rose from her seat. She remained calm in the face of everyone watching, but she would not sit there a moment longer.

"Sit. Down." Vince growled.

She remained standing.

"Kara, if you don't want to see your *boyfriends* all behind bars for the rest of their lives, you will sit down, and *listen*." He kept his voice low, but his own anger boiled under the surface of his red face.

She reluctantly sat. She folded her shaking hands on her lap beneath the table.

"This is what you will do. You will end your *whore ways, immediately*. You will go to them and end this *farce* of a relationship. You will tell them you can no longer help them with the Granger case, then you will *stop digging into things you don't belong in*," he ordered vehemently. "Do you understand me?"

"Yes, Father," she answered sardonically and rolled her eyes.

He glared at her, dropping all pretenses for the crowd behind her. He eyed her carefully before he nodded. "You may go." He waved a hand at her dismissively.

She didn't hesitate. She glared at him, grabbed her purse, and left. She didn't need to be told twice.

# Chapter Seventeen

It was another night Kara spent crying alone. She didn't bother to reach out to her guys. There was no point. They had made it clear that they didn't have time for her this week. After a weekend fuckfest, they were done with her.

Her father had made it clear that her whore ways would only lead to them being imprisoned.

She didn't put it past him. Not after everything he had revealed. Not after the things she's helped him bury over the years. Her father was not a good man. She had known that from the start. And like a fool, she'd let him rope her into this false sense of security with him, as if she were desperate for love.

Now she was well and truly *fucked*.

She didn't bother going to work that day. It was Friday, her schedule was mostly empty. She texted her secretary and called off.

She spent most of her morning crying and debating with herself.

Her heart was broken. She'd fallen in love with her three men in the course of the last two months. It had been a whirlwind romance from the start, but there was no way they could last long-term. Not if they didn't put in any effort. And the past week only went to show that they couldn't be bothered.

She was a grown-ass woman. She didn't need to wait around for some men to decide she was worth their time.

She made her decision. She resolved herself to the consequences and set about showering and getting herself ready.

Kevin texted while she was in the shower, and she had to shake her head at the universe's timing. **Hey, baby. Sorry we've been MIA this week. We'll explain when we see you. Why don't you come by the clubhouse tonight after work?**

It was two in the afternoon. She decided to bite the bullet and head to the clubhouse early. Hopefully there would be fewer people around to witness the fallout.

An hour later, dressed in a suit for the office, she pulled up into the yard of the clubhouse, with its multiple buildings and lines of bikes. There were more bikes than usual in the yard, and the gates had been closed when she pulled up. Thankfully Vagabond had been at the gate and let her through without a fuss.

The air was charged, and everyone seemed on edge.

She looked around and only saw unfamiliar faces loitering around. She headed into the clubhouse building and had to wait for her eyes to adjust to the dim lighting.

"There she is," Derrick called out from across the semibusy room. He was playing pool with a couple guys she didn't recognize, but she saw Johnny and Kevin through the open double doors to church.

Johnny looked weary, but Kevin smiled when he saw her.

Kara headed toward them, scanning the patches on the men who loitered around the room. San Jose, Oakland, Las Vegas, Salt Lake City, Cheyenne, Boulder, Omaha, Cedar Rapids. She took it all in quickly as she moved toward church.

Something was clearly going on. She felt guilty for what she was about to do to them.

Kevin walked around the long conference table, passing Johnny, and met her in the doorway. He leaned down to kiss her. Last minute she turned her head so he kissed her cheek instead. "Oh, you're pissed." Kevin chuckled. "Got it."

She waited until Derrick walked in and closed the doors behind him. He wrapped his arms around her from behind and pressed an open-mouthed kiss to her neck. "God, I missed you," he breathed into her skin.

She closed her eyes and reveled in the warmth of his touch, but she didn't lean into him like she usually would. She kept her hands on the back of the chair she stood before and willed herself not to cry.

Her heart pounded in her chest. Breathing was hard, but she had to get through this. When Derrick pulled away and walked around the other side of the table, Kevin spoke up. "We're really sorry about this week. Let's sit and we'll tell you all about it."

Kara watched Johnny sit at the head of the table while Kevin and Derrick took the spots on either side of him.

She slowly took the seat next to Kevin, the one she was standing in front of.

"What's going on, Kara?" Johnny asked as she sat down. He had been watching her warily, his blue eyes guarded. She didn't miss the fact that he purposely used her name and not his nickname for her.

She steeled herself and met his hard gaze. "I'm sorry," she started, "but I have to end things."

Johnny immediately shook his head in disbelief while Derrick hissed. Only Kevin sat there emotionless and stared at her. "What, we didn't give you enough attention this week?" Johnny goaded. "Little whore not get enough?"

Kara ignored his comments. "My father is stepping in to take over the Granger case against your father," she continued. "I can no longer help Mac with the case."

"Can't or won't?" Johnny growled.

Kara closed her eyes briefly and braced herself for the final blow. "I won't go against my father," she answered plainly, meeting his steely gaze.

"Jesus *fucking* Christ," Johnny spat and got to his feet. "You really are just like every other loose pussy out there." He flung his hand out toward the clubhouse. "Maybe I should have just let the rest of my brothers have their way with you. You really would be just like the rest of the sluts then."

Kara didn't respond. Her heart broke watching him lash out. She slowly got to her feet.

Kevin and Derrick stared at the table until she stood up. They both looked resigned and angry but didn't say anything. "I'm sorry," she said to the room.

"Yeah, go on, git!" he shouted at her. "Just another whore to walk through these halls. You're a dime a dozen."

Kara let his words wash over her as she opened the door and walked out. She ignored all the club members that looked over when she exited church. She was grateful for her decision to wear a business suit. It felt like a layer of armor against the hungry stares.

She didn't know how much they had heard, nor did she care.

This would be the last time she ever stepped foot in the clubhouse.

"JOHNNY, WHAT THE FUCK man." Derrick groaned after Kara had walked out of the room and out of their lives. Johnny shook his head.

"Something happened," Kevin spoke up, shaking his head in disbelief. "Something has her spooked."

Johnny laughed sardonically. "Nah, that's every slut after we ignore them for a week. It's typical whore behavior. If their pussies aren't being pounded, they lose their brains."

"Dude, don't fucking talk about her like that," Kevin snapped and stood from the table.

Derrick ran his hands through his shoulder-length mane and sighed. "Kevin's right. This isn't Kara."

Johnny shook his head. "Doesn't matter if it is or not. She ended it and we have bigger fish to fry. Use some courtesan to get your dicks wet," he spat before he stormed out of church.

Kara spent the night and most of Saturday crying in her bed. Her heart was broken. She had fallen in love with all three of them so fast and so fiercely. She felt lost knowing it was over.

It had to be over, though. Her father would stick to his promise of having them arrested for something they didn't do. Look at what he was doing to Mac, a man he admitted had been his best friend at one time.

It was late Saturday evening when Kara dried her tears and resolved herself to her actions. She ordered Chinese takeout to be delivered and settled in on the couch, snuggled up in a blanket. She turned on some stupid rom-com and zoned out.

She was half asleep when she heard a scuffle at the front door. Thinking it was the delivery guy, she got up, grabbed her wallet from the kitchen, and headed for the door. The door opened before she could reach it, though, and she froze, thinking it was maybe one of her guys.

The big burly man was definitely *not* one of her boys. He was dressed in black from head to toe. A black ski mask covered his face and only allowed for a sliver of his eyes to show. He certainly was not the deliveryman either.

How the fuck did he get through her locked door?

She didn't stick around to find out. She quickly spun on her heels and ran toward the kitchen. Her socks slipped on the hardwood floor, and her attacker wrapped a hand in her ponytail and yanked her backward. She landed sprawled on her back with the wind knocked out of her. Her head hit, leaving her dazed as she struggled to get oxygen into her lungs.

Her attacker was fast and quickly pinned her down by straddling her waist. He was easily twice her size both physically and by weight. She didn't see the punch coming before it was too late, and pain bloomed across her cheek.

She managed to twist before the next punch hit. She got her forearm up in time and blocked it. At the same time, she got in a quick jab to his junk.

The man groaned and curved to cover his jewels. She used his momentum to twitch her hips and throw him off her. She scrambled to her feet and raced to the kitchen. She grabbed a knife out of the butcher block before her attacker was on her again.

She whirled and swung the knife wide.

"Fucking bitch," the man growled when she sliced through flesh. She had managed to cut open his arm.

She went on the offensive and stabbed forward. He dodged and grabbed her wrist, wrenching it. He squeezed so hard she felt like her bones were bending. She cried out in pain. Her grip on the knife released, and it fell to the hardwood floor with a clatter.

She struck out with her foot to kick him in the balls again, but he smacked her leg out of the way, sending her body turning away. He moved forward at the same time, and her other foot got caught up between his legs. He shoved her down roughly, and she heard a loud pop in her left knee as she twisted and fell down.

She screamed in agony. She tried to curl forward to grab her injured leg, but his knee came up and slammed into her face.

She groaned as pain radiated across her face. She didn't feel anything crunch, but blood immediately poured from her nose in thick clots before it ran smoothly down her face.

She was a mess. All of her self-defense training had gone out the window. She needed a weapon. Or an escape route. Her thoughts were jumbled; she could barely think. She struggled to back away from the man towering over her.

She whimpered as she inched backward.

He silently advanced.

Her back hit something. She looked away from her attacker, startled to be cornered. It was a door, though. The basement door. Her attacker was still ten feet away. She struggled to her feet. Her knee screamed in agony. Kara cried out and used the doorknob to pull herself up to her good leg.

She remembered the exit to the garage in the basement and swung open the door. She tried to quickly close and lock it behind her, but her attacker was once again faster. He grabbed her wrist and twisted it painfully. She pivoted on her good knee and managed to land an elbow to his gut.

He grunted and bent over. She landed another elbow, this time to his nose. He growled as it crunched. "Fucking bitch!" He howled in pain and fell backward on his ass.

"Fuck off, asshole," she grumbled and turned toward the stairs again.

She didn't see his foot swing out and kick her feet out from under her. She cried out as her world tilted and her stomach dropped. Her arms flailed, trying to find something to grab on to. But it was too late. She was falling.

She tried to curl her body to fall defensively, but it didn't matter. She fell hard down the unfinished wooden stairs. Her body landed in a crumpled heap on the concrete floor at the bottom. Her ribs crunched upon impact, and she felt something in her wrist give way.

She took a gasping breath, wondering why it felt like she was trying to breathe underwater. The last thing she saw before her world went black was her attacker slowly descending the stairs.

She came to, to the smell of acrid smoke in the air. She looked around in a daze. She was still at the bottom of the stairs. The basement was filled with smoke. Flames roared across the ceiling.

She heard footsteps approaching and looked up the stairs.

Her attacker was slowly walking down the steps. A black handgun was held out in front of him.

Kara struggled to back away. She used her elbows to drag her body backward. She winced when her elbow hit something metal. She looked quickly and saw the iron poker for her fireplace.

She picked it up and gripped it as hard as she could with her left hand—her right wrist appeared to be broken.

She didn't know why her attacker hadn't shot her yet. He advanced toward her, and she swung out with the poker with all her might. It hit him on the arm and, by some miracle, knocked the gun out of his hand.

She used every ounce of strength she had left to sit up and grab the gun before he could bend down for it.

She flicked off the safety, aimed, and squeezed the trigger, all with her left hand, before she could even think of aiming correctly. It didn't matter. The man was large and three feet from her. She squeezed the trigger several more times, hitting him in the chest.

She fired until the gun was out of bullets and she realized she was screaming.

Her attacker fell backward, sprawled out at the bottom of the stairs.

She struggled to her good knee and hobbled toward him. She needed to know who he was. She reached for the ski mask and pulled it off his face. Staring back at her was the gaping mouth of Randall Diggins.

Her father's hired goon.

She watched Diggins take his last breath and the light dim from his eyes before she fell away from him panting.

Her father had tried to kill her even after he'd ordered her to quit digging. Whatever her father was hiding, he would rather kill his own daughter than let it get out.

Kara coughed as smoke filled the basement. Her vision was darkening. She gave in to the darkness, too tired to move.

# Chapter Nineteen

JOHNNY RODE AROUND MOURNINGSIDE, his head a mess. How the fuck could Kara just walk in and stomp all over his heart with a few simple words? Why the fuck did he even care?

How the fuck had he fallen for her so quickly?

He didn't let himself get attached to women. Ever. He didn't fall in love with some whore.

But Kara wasn't just some whore. No. Kara was special. Kara stood up to him. Kara gave as good as she got. She was fiery and passionate. She wasn't afraid to stick up for herself and didn't back down from a fight.

Then why the fuck did she just sit there and take everything he threw at her in church? Why didn't she fight back? Call him out for talking to her like that?

Why the hell did she walk away so easily?

Johnny's anger only grew the farther he rode. He didn't even remember making the turns toward Kara's house, but when he was blocks from her home, he knew he had to talk to her. Why the fuck would she just leave them like that?

The closer he got, the more he smelled the acrid scent of smoke. Something was on fire. Something large.

He turned the corner to her block and cussed. Her beautiful blue Craftsman was completely engulfed in flames.

He made a split-second decision and parked the bike several houses down. He stripped off his cut and left it on his bike before he ran toward her house. He kicked open the side door to the garage and headed for the stairs in the back that led to the basement.

The garage was still untouched. He hoped like hell he could get through the basement door leading into the kitchen. Smoke filled the air as he descended the stairs. He lifted his shirt over his nose and crouched down.

The door at the bottom opened easily, and he ran inside. He had to crouch low in the basement. The smoke was thick and black. It was dark and hard to see. He made his way across the room from memory of the layout alone.

He stumbled when he reached the bottom of the stairs that led up to the kitchen. There were two bodies lying on the floor at the base of the steps. Two unmoving bodies.

"Kara!" Johnny shouted when he realized the smaller body was hers.

He reached out and put his fingers on her neck. "Thank God." He groaned when he felt her pulse. It was faint, but it was there.

A quick glance at the other body showed several gunshot wounds to the chest. Johnny couldn't even begin to fathom what had happened here. He didn't have time to think about it, though; he had to get Kara out.

"Come on, baby," he muttered as he slid his hands beneath her back and knees.

He lifted her easily into his arms. Smoke clouded his vision. He started coughing.

"Fucking hell," he groaned and rushed toward the garage stairs.

He stumbled down the driveway toward the front yard. Sirens wailed in the distance.

People were starting to come out of their homes.

Kara groaned as he set her down. Her hand came up to his face. Her fingers scratched through his beard. "Johnny?" she mumbled.

"Shh, Princess," he whispered. "Hang on. Help is coming."

He couldn't stay. He saw the flashing lights in the distance and cursed. He pressed a kiss to her forehead and left her there.

He ran for his bike and disappeared before the ambulance pulled to a stop in front of Kara's house.

He could only hope he had gotten there in time.

## To Be Continued...

Reconciling the Consequences

Ravagers Knights MC book 2, will be released January 1st, 2024.

Pre-order today!

To my loving husband... your support has been constant and the foundation that allowed me to follow my dreams. From every meal you cooked, to every bedtime with the kids you handled on your own while I met with a writing group, or met a deadline, you have handled without complaint—mostly —and with support. You are my rock and home, always. I love you.

To my best friend, Rachel. Thank you for ALWAYS being my best friend and sister. Your constant support and guidance have been a life-saver over the many years of our friendship. You're always willing to listen to me bather on about writing or life in general. While I've ranted and raved, or whined and cried, you've always supported me without judgment—or with some much needed—and loved me unconditionally. I love you girl.

To my author friend Jessica Baker, thank you for the countless hours of support, brain storm sessions, and encouragement. Thank you for every single piece of wisdom, advice and guidance you've offered me throughout not only the publishing process, but in life in general. Your knowledge and friendship have been an absolute blessing. I will cherish our friendship always.

To my beta readers! Rachel, Megan, April, and Jessica! Thank you SO so much, from the bottom of my heart! I really appreciate your thoughts and feedback. Love you ladies always!

M.E. Thornwood is a contemporary romance author, who enjoys writing about dark themes, thrilling suspense, and hot hot spice. She loves her alpha males and the women who don't put up with them. Writing has been her passion since she was a little girl.

She lives in the Midwest with her husband and two children. When she's not writing, she's enjoying camping and hiking with family and friends, crafting with her kids, and reading books with her loveable fat cat Midnight.

www.ingramcontent.com/pod-product-compliance
Lightning Source LLC
Chambersburg PA
CBHW022128310726
48972CB00007B/2247